THE NUREYEV
VALENTINO

W9-DDN-526

A DELTA SPECIAL

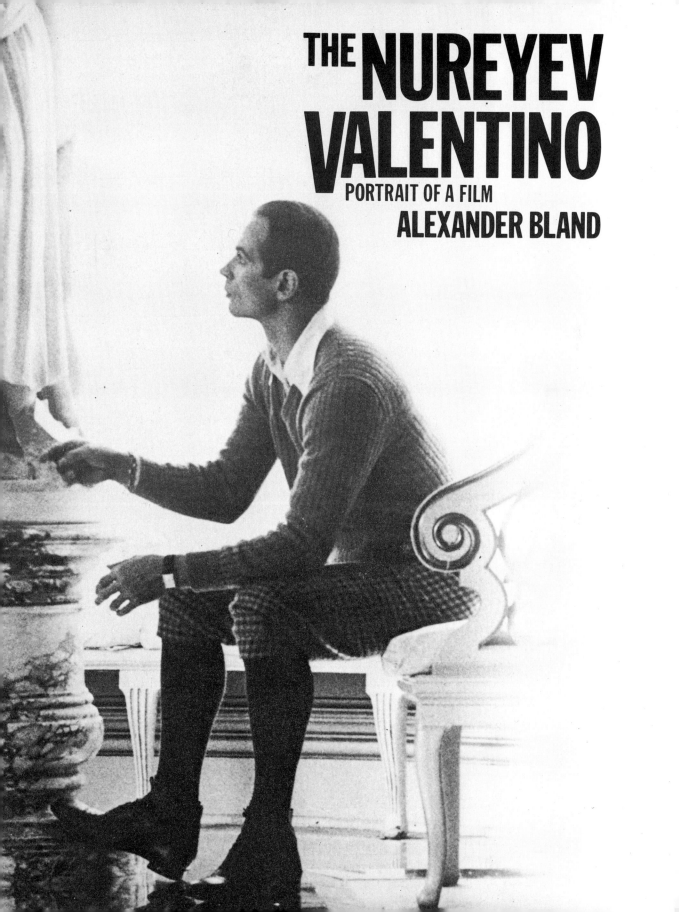

THE NUREYEV VALENTINO

PORTRAIT OF A FILM

ALEXANDER BLAND

When this book was first suggested, in the final phases of shooting, it seemed an impossible project – especially since Ken Russell had from the beginning promised himself to make no comment on his work. That it materialized is due to the generous cooperation of everybody connected with the film and to the tenacity and enthusiasm of Tristram Holland of Studio Vista – to all of whom my thanks.   A.B.

All the photographs that appear in this book were taken by Barry Peake © United Artists Corporation 1977, with the following exceptions: on pages 16-17, 23, 27, 29, 30, 33, 58 *below,* 63, 93 *above right,* 94 *above* by Lenny Pollack © United Artists Corporation 1977; on pages 18, 24-25, 28, 41, 80, 126-127 by David Steen © United Artists Corporation 1977; on pages 35, 68 *above,* 84 *below* details from frames from the film © United Artists Corporation 1977; on page 20 by Alan Cunliffe; on page 21 by Frederika Davis; on pages 6 *left,* 9 *left,* 10, 14 *left,* 15 *left* from the Kobal Collection; on page 12 from the collection of Maurice Beck and Helen MacGregor by courtesy of Weidenfeld & Nicholson.

A DELTA SPECIAL

Published by
Dell Publishing Co., Inc.
1 Dag Hammarskjold Plaza
New York, New York 10017

Copyright © 1977 by Alexander Bland

All rights reserved. No part of this book may be reproduced in any form or by any means without the prior written permission of Dell Publishing Co., Inc., New York, N.Y. 10017, excepting brief quotes used in connection with reviews written specifically for inclusion in a magazine or newspaper.

Published by arrangement with Studio Vista, a division of Cassell & Collier Macmillan Publishers Ltd

Delta® TM 755118, Dell Publishing Co., Inc.

Manufactured in Great Britain

First Delta printing — October 1977

CONTENTS

Bringing a legend back to life   6

Rudolf as Rudolph   16

The Russell treatment   38

Shooting the stars   50

Cast list and technical credits   65

The Valentino story   66

BRINGING A LEGEND BACK TO LIFE

In August 1926 the screen actor Rudolph Valentino died in New York at the age of thirty-one. Almost exactly fifty years later, in August 1976, the cameras began to roll again for a film with his name on the title sheet. The alchemy of art had brought about a strange rebirth. The Sheik carrying a half-reluctant maiden into his tent went through familiar motions, but he bore another name. Rudolph had turned into Rudolf, Valentino became Nureyev. On Spanish sands a Russian tartar was reincarnating an Italian in the role of an Arab. The portrayer of screen heroes had himself become a screen hero, a star impersonated by a star.

It was an occasion in which Valentino would surely have felt at home. The first great romantic superstar of the cinema, his image still haunts its history. Half hero and half victim, triumphant, battered (the American male, threatened by the success of his foreign charms, hit back by accusations of effeminacy and hints of impotence), sometimes pathetic but never pitiable, armed with a charisma which nothing could impair, he makes an obvious subject for a film.

Valentino was conceived – appropriately in Hollywood – in the minds of a pair of producers, Robert Chartoff and Irwin Winkler, partners for eleven years and godfathers to twenty pictures. 'Every year we are reminded of Valentino in Los Angeles by the commemoration held at his crypt,' says Chartoff. 'He opens the lid on a whole period; he's part of our legend and lore, the first great romantic leading man, the Great Lover. He's never left our sight or mind and he probably never will.

Left
Rudolph Valentino does the celebrated tango with Beatrice Dominguez in *The Four Horsemen of the Apocalypse*.

Right
Nureyev and Christine Carlson, wearing costumes almost identical with the originals, in a tango scene in the Russell film.

'We have informal meetings every week, Irwin, myself and our associate Gene Kirkwood, and we began to examine the potential of a film project on his life. What excited us was the idea of Valentino as the first personality created by the mass media instrument in its infancy, and the inconsistency between his own life and his screen persona, between the real Rudolph and the fantasy Valentino. Also there was the realisation that this was an authentic legend which had started in our parents' lifetime, almost like a Greek myth which happened yesterday.

'So we engaged Mardek Martin, a talented writer with a strong feeling for the material, to research the facts and write a screenplay. The story came out pretty well as we had anticipated, one of contradictions, of a Great Lover who was personally very confused about that role and of a simple immigrant who seemed attracted almost irresistably to glamour, like metal being drawn by a magnet. We could see we had a film.

'We brought our ideas and enthusiasm, along with Mardek's outline of his story, to our financiers, United Artists, who were all as enthusiastic as we were and encouraged us with their support. We knew we were on to something.'

The next stage to get the movie going was to find a director. 'One name came to mind immediately. We decided straight away that Ken Russell was just the man to delve into the subtleties and paradoxes of the Valentino legend, to look behind the known facts to the more hidden and subjective elements. We knew Russell's films and admired them; to us he was the obvious choice. We contacted him and told him of our approach and immediately he agreed to participate in our project.'

'I had heard that Russell could be difficult so I was a bit nervous before our first meeting in London,' admits Winkler. 'But he invited us to dinner and as soon as he heard our ideas he seemed fascinated. He particularly liked our idea, based on actual information, of a scene in the funeral parlor where the real body of Valentino would be lying upstairs on a cake of ice, to preserve it in the heat of August in New York, while all his fans and friends and associates would be fussing over a wax replica. But you know how things are in films – in the end the whole wax idea was dropped.'

Chartoff continues the story. 'While Russell was doing his research he came on some Valentino lore indicating that he actually taught the tango to Nijinsky when both young men were in New York. We all agreed that this would make a dynamic visual and sensual introduction to *Valentino*. We planned to start the film with the funeral and proceed in flashbacks through the memories of the people close to him. Then Russell said: "I know who should play Nijinsky – Nureyev. But it's only a two-day part; could we persuade him to do it?" So we rang Nureyev's agent who thought it was actually possible that he might consider this small role if he was sufficiently intrigued by the challenge. We spoke to Nureyev

Left
Rudolph Valentino in *Blood and Sand*.

Right
Nureyev as Valentino in his matador costume.

and his reply was, "Yes. If I can fit it in, I'll do it." We had our Nijinsky – the only casting we had done at that point.

'Then we had to begin to find someone to play Valentino himself. We didn't know where to look. We went through the usual list of leading men from A to Z and we found many who had marvellous qualities but no one who would ignite the spark of enthusiasm. We could not find the man who would represent the whole story as we saw it – the mystery, the legend, the tragedy. We also considered using a less-known actor, and we saw several young men who were possible, but never the real answer. We even speculated on what Valentino would be doing if he were alive today. He might well be working in an Italian restaurant in London, rather than in the dance halls of New York, and we thought of checking out the trattorias. We were desperate.

'Then suddenly Russell suggested "Why not our Nijinsky?" And immediately it became clear that Nureyev was the living symbol of what Valentino was all about. He was the perfect man for the part. It just had to be Nureyev.' So the script was sent to the dancer and Russell and Chartoff arranged to meet him in Amsterdam. 'There was no doubt in any of our minds as the evening ended that the part was his.'

The next important problem was Nureyev's availability. He

was booked for a year, but it was decided that he was worth the waiting. Russell started an extensive re-writing of the script, with Nureyev in mind and incorporating his own approach to the story, while his wife, Shirley, designed the costumes and Philip Harrison worked on the sets.

'Meanwhile we had to cast the picture, to find people to play all those great figures of the cast. There was Natasha Rambova, Valentino's second wife – perhaps worthy of a movie biography herself. She was a brilliant avant garde personality who exerted a powerful effect on his life in his prime years, when her own ambitions were interwoven with his. And Nazimova, a fascinating larger-than-life actress, an innovator herself in her early years; and George Ullman, Valentino's faithful agent. The casting was arduous – more so than in any picture I have worked on. It lasted until the day we began shooting – indeed even while we were shooting.

'The day, you know you are actually starting a film is when the screenplay is brought to the point where it is artistically correct and can be assessed and budgeted. In the case of *Valentino* we were faced with daily operating costs in excess of $25,000 and a total budget of $5,000,000.

'The idea of working with two men both famous for their flamboyant personalities was a great fascination for me, bringing both opportunities and pitfalls. I knew they would have to work together on a daily basis – both very temperamental in their own ways, as artists must be. I felt my own function was to be there moderating between these two very strong forces.

'As I saw it, the task of the film was to explore the character of Valentino as seen by his historians, as he appears in his movies, as he looked to his contemporaries, as he was reconceived by Russell and, finally, as he was interpreted by Nureyev. Every artist brings something of himself into a character and Nureyev brought much of his own mystery and romance into Valentino. Russell gave him a great deal of freedom to redefine the character, and it was fascinating to watch this happening. As a dancer Nureyev is an interpretative artist, he doesn't just do the steps or the set roles – that is part of his greatness in his chosen field; and it proved to be true in his adopted field as well. He is an innovator and a creator and I think he saw parallels between his own life and Valentino's. He dealt with Valentino's emotional problems as he himself would deal with them, which proved a big bonus for us, for we had never imagined the complexities and intelligence that he could bring to the character. With all the scriptwriting that was done, it was the man himself, Nureyev, whose intuition and instincts led us to understand our own Valentino.'

What are the facts about this character they were trying to recreate? Even in his lifetime they were fogged by clouds of gossip and publicists' invention; after his death witnesses were mostly swayed by sentiment or self-interest. His own autobiographical 'Diary', cobbled up for a magazine, is deeply

Rudolph Valentino and Agnes Ayres in a scene from *The Sheik*.

In a tent prepared for Russell's version of _The Sheik,_ Valentino (Nureyev) and Rambova (Michelle Phillips) play a love scene of their own.

suspect. Surprisingly few reliable details survive.

Rudolph was his real name but Valentino was not. He was born on 6 May 1895 on a farm in a village called Castellaneta, near Taranto in Southern Italy, and was christened Rudolpho Alfonzo Raffaelo Pierre Filibert Guglielmi di Valentina d'Antonguolla.

His father died while he was still a boy and the young Rudolpho Guglielmi left his French-born mother, his brother Alberto and his two sisters Beatrice and Maria, to attend college. On leaving he tried to enter the Naval Academy but was rejected on physical grounds (his chest was too small and all his life he was to be obsessed with physical culture). Instead he found himself at a less glamorous school of agriculture. He was far from a model pupil, more interested in gym exercises and dancing classes, but he eventually received his diploma.

On leaving he may have paid a visit to Paris. He certainly developed a taste for cheerful company and smart clothes and acquired social ambitions. In December 1913 he sailed for America to join the new flood of Italian immigrants in the search for fame and fortune. He was eighteen and shipboard photographs show him as a dashing, well-turned out youth with a trim figure, a handsome smile and a clean white handkerchief.

Once in America, he found it harder to get work than he had probably anticipated. He had to be content with humble jobs like gardener and waiter. It was his restaurant connections which were to prove the key to his future. His good looks and winning manners won him a job as a paid partner or 'gigolo' in one of the tea-rooms where ladies used to spend their time on the dance floor while their husbands were in their offices – a harmless but daring novelty symptomatic of the new-found independence of American women. Rudolph di Valentina, as he now called himself, was tall, sophisticated and dark-skinned, with a classical profile. Inclined to put on weight, he was already at twenty wearing a corset – a garment less unusual at the time than his wrist-watch, which aroused suspicions of effeminacy. But clearly his dancing was exceptional. He claimed to have been asked by Diaghilev to give lessons in the tango to Nijinsky himself, and he found immense favour with the ladies. Soon he had become the professional partner of a well-known demonstration dancer, Bonnie Glass.

Touring as a professional dancer became his regular job. He was engaged by another partner after Miss Glass retired and then joined the cast of two musical shows, *The Masked Model* and *Nobody Home*. In 1918, at the age of twenty-three, he moved to Los Angeles and got his first film engagement – dancing again, as an extra in a ballroom scene in *Alimony*. Still appearing from time to time to dance in night-clubs, he played small roles in several films, usually cast as the villain – his smoochy Latin looks seemed unsuitable for the healthy heroes popular in America. But in 1920 a well-known Metro Goldywn Mayer scriptwriter, June Mathis, was looking for someone to play the lead in a Spanish story she had just adapted from a novel by Blasco-Ibanez, *The Four Horsemen of the Apocalypse*. As Julio, the playboy hero turned into a man by wartime suffering, was supposed to be Latin-American she recommended the almost unknown young actor. Rex Ingram recognized his talent, built up the part and directed him with understanding skill. Valentino (as he had become by now) was a sensation; his sultry love-making swept female audiences off their feet.

No actor had ever had such an instant and devastating success, and from then on his career was a triumph. Inevitably he became trapped by his own achievement, particularly after *The Sheik* (1921) in which his particular gift of exuding a combination of menace, courtesy and sensuality reached an apex in a story which he himself despised. His image as the Great Screen Lover obstinately stood in the way of his efforts to widen his range and exploit his acting talent.

The public wanted him in fancy costume and they wanted him to satisfy their sado-masochist dreams; comedy, realistic contemporary drama or sophistication were unacceptable. Films like *Moran of the Lady Letty, Beyond the Rocks, Sainted*

Rudolph Valentino poses as Nijinsky in *L'après-midi d'un faune.*

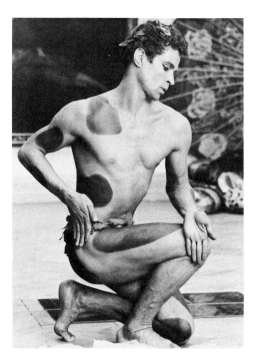

**Nureyev as Valentino imitating Nijinsky in
*L'après-midi d'un faune.***

Devil and *Cobra* made no impression; even the high-camp artifice of *Monsieur Beaucaire* failed at the box office. But *Blood and Sand, The Young Rajah, The Eagle,* and *Son of the Sheik* stamped his glamour ineffaceably onto the screen.

As Valentino's fame grew, his ambitions rose and he became more and more discontented. He quarrelled with his employers, switched from MGM to Columbia, and from Columbia to a producer called Ritz-Carlton. He spent his earnings extravagantly, riding in specially designed French cars, keeping a string of horses at his expensively designed home, lavishly furnished with antiques picked up on trips to Europe, indulging in his love of dressing up and foppishness. He was in debt, artistically frustrated and lonely.

For his private life was increasingly unsatisfactory. He seems to have lacked the sexual drive which pushed some Hollywood stars into scandals, but was equally unsuited to domesticity. He was evidently attracted to strong, dominating women, and this led him into a lesbian set. When he was only twenty-four and still unknown he married a young actress called Jean Acker, a close friend of a famous Russian actress, the reigning star of MGM, Alla Nazimova. She locked Valentino out of the bedroom after the wedding and the marriage was soon annulled.

He promptly became the protégé of the thirty-nine year old June Mathis, who had scripted three of Nazimova's films. She seems to have had no romantic interest in Valentino but it was she, together with Nazimova and a young friend, Natasha Rambova, who picked him out for stardom and she remained one of his most faithful friends, as well as scripting four of his films.

But the most decisive influence in Valentino's life was Rambova. Born Winnifred Shaughnessy, she became the stepdaughter of a rich perfume tycoon. She had travelled in Europe and spoke perfect French, learnt dancing with a Russian ballet master and developed into a stage designer of genuine talent – her designs for Nazimova's homosexual production of Oscar Wilde's *Salome* look impressive even today. 'She had as much poise as Valentino', wrote the photographer Abbé . . . 'She was reserved, educated, refined and nicely sophisticated.' She and Nazimova made a powerful pair who wielded huge influence in Hollywood. She attached herself to Valentino, who fell completely under her spell. After legal difficulties and even a brief imprisonment over his divorce from Jean Acker, he married her and she decided to take charge of his career. She encouraged him to quarrel with his studio, to demand more money and more 'artistic' films. Eventually, after violent scenes over *Monsieur Beaucaire,* she overplayed her hand. George Ullman, Valentino's new manager, arranged to have her official powers curtailed; Valentino became restive; and she walked off – with her marriage apparently still unconsummated.

These sterile relationships added to the gossip about Valen-

The old gaucho and the new — Rudolph Valentino *(left)* and Nureyev *(right)*.

tino's lack of masculinity. Virile American men resented his boudoir charms and a steady barrage of snide innuendo began to circulate, insinuating that he was a homosexual. Valentino tried to fight off the attack by public demonstrations of prowess in riding, boxing, fencing and other manly pursuits, but a chance article in a Chicago gossip column, suggesting that American manhood was being undermined by a hero who used a powder puff in the men's room, brought matters to a head.

To an Italian such a public slur on his honour was unforgiveable. Valentino was beside himself. He (unsuccessfully) challenged the journalist to meet him in the boxing ring, and even secretly visited the highly respected writer H. L. Mencken for fatherly advice. Mencken was apparently touched by his simple and dignified naiveté. After noting his very wide braces, he conceded that Valentino had a touch of the gentleman about him. 'His agony was the agony of a man of relatively civilized feelings thrown into a situation of intolerable vulgarity.' He advised him gently to dismiss the whole trivial matter, but he could not. He was already unwell and the nervous strain taxed him even more. He suddenly became seriously ill from gastric

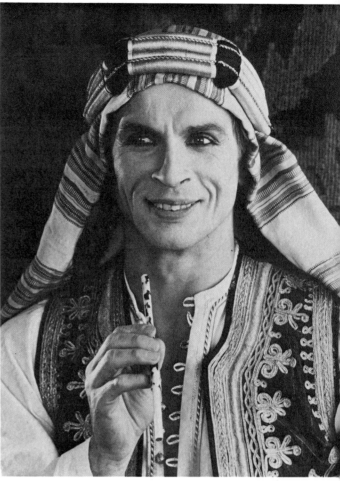

Rudolph Valentino *(left)* **and Nureyev** *(right)*
in their respective Sheik costumes.

trouble. The story of his collapse filled the headlines and the new radio networks spread the bulletins across the world. On 22 August 1926 the incredible announcement came. 'Rudi' was dead.

The sequel was almost frightening. The newspapers had a field day (one of them depicted Valentino being received in heaven by the singer Caruso) and mobs filled the streets outside the funeral parlor where the body lay. Within a few days 100,000 people filed past his powdered and painted corpse. A hundred were injured in the struggle to gain admittance and his leading ladies competed to hog the camera in front of the coffin. The film tycoons were appalled at the disappearance of their dollar-earner. The fans were inconsolable. The man was dead. But the legend had been born, and lay waiting for somebody to incarnate it.

RUDOLF AS RUDOLPH

The question which faced Ken Russell when he decided to tackle the story boiled down to a personal one: who should play Valentino? Mere facial resemblance would not be enough, as several unsuccessful attempts had shown. What was needed was somebody with the same sexual glamour that Valentino had exuded, the same magnetism, the same mysterious power to hit theatrically below the belt.

That the answer should turn out to be a dancer is not altogether surprising. Valentino's first break-through into public attention had been on the dance-floor and he reverted to the role of dancing-partner even at the height of his career. His first film success, in *The Four Horsemen of the Apocalypse*, rested partly on a striking tango sequence and his whole style had a sense of the ballet hero, strong but supple, controlled, feline. He even posed for some private pictures in the costume of Nijinsky's *L'Après midi d'un faune* and claimed to have taught the Russian star how to tango.

Dance was also Russell's first – abortive – profession, and it shows in all his work. 'Russell's dance background is fifty per cent of his directing technique,' says Leslie Caron (herself first celebrated as a ballet dancer), who plays Nazimova in *Valentino*. 'Most directors start from the text. With Russell it's all visual – the composition and the movements inside it, the camera movements, the lighting as though for a ballet set.' 'He wants to keep everything moving,' adds Seymour Cassell, who plays Ullman, Valentino's manager, and Russell himself freely admits this tendancy: 'All my films are choreography,' he has said. 'There's no reason why a dancer . . . shouldn't be good in a dramatic role. In a way dancing is greater than acting with words, because you're conveying emotions and ideas without words. In a lot of my films it's the atmosphere I'm after . . . in some of them you *need* to dance.'

Nureyev as Valentino.

17

And sure enough, Russell has always included dance sequences in his films and chosen dancers for actors. Christopher Gable, a star of the Royal Ballet, was one of his first leading men and the cast of *Valentino* includes not only Leslie but three other figures well known in the dance world – Anthony Dowell, the finest British male dancer of his generation, Lindsay Kemp, choreographer and mime-dancer, and Leland Palmer who made her reputation in New York musicals.

He could hardly miss Nureyev, who is no ordinary dancer. He has somehow broken through the barrier round the arts to become, like Valentino, familiar far outside his own particular world. An uncanny similarity binds, below the surface, the apparently dissimilar figures of the dark Italian and the fair-skinned Russian. Both chose to leave their homeland and seek fame and fortune among strangers. Both succeeded almost beyond their dreams. The fire, sensuality and romance which Nureyev injected into ballet produced the same shock-waves as those generated by Valentino's film allure. But both were subjected to pressures and practices to which they were completely unaccustomed. The commercial exploitation and pitiless publicity which tormented Valentino are not strangers to Nureyev. He knows at first hand both the rewards and the penalties of international fame. He does not have to act in order to move through a crowd like a star, or endure the adulation of hysterical admirers. The love-hate relationship between a fictional hero and his fans is something he knows only too well. When, in the film, Valentino parts the curtains to look out at a sea of chanting teenagers it is Nureyev too facing his admirers. The role and the player seem to have been waiting for each other.

Nureyev was born in Siberia, in a train speeding eastwards. His pregnant mother was travelling with her three small daughters to visit her husband. Where the line passes between the Lake Baikal and the mountains of Mongolia, the baby began to arrive. On 17th March 1938 Rudolf Hametovitch Nureyev made a characteristically unorthodox entry into the world.

Both his parents were of Tartar stock. They came from Bashkiria, in southern Russia, and it was there that Nureyev passed his childhood, near the provincial centre of Ufa. His father was away with the army, and life was cruelly hard, with poverty exaggerated by the austerities of wartime. Nureyev recalls that his only solace was listening to the radio.

His other escape was into dancing, for which he developed a passion. After a chance visit to the Ufa opera house to see a ballet he became determined to be a dancer. Through sheer persistence he wormed his way on to the stage in Ufa as an extra, persuaded an elderly ex-ballerina to give him some lessons in the rudiments of the classical technique, and finally got himself accepted into the famous dance school in Leningrad where Pavlova and Nijinsky had trained.

Once there his progress was phenomenal, though stormy; he

Russell watches Nureyev rehearsing a tense moment on the dance floor.

Opposite
Felicity Kendal and Nureyev in a scene which was eventually cut — a gaucho tango fantasy.

Nureyev as the rebellious hero of Balanchine's ballet, *The Prodigal Son*. A characteristically fiery and spectacular leap.

disconcerted his fellow students by his fanatical hard work and offended the authorities by his obstinate non-conformity. But nothing could stop his talent. Within three years he had completed the whole course and in 1958 he was accepted as a soloist by the world-famous Kirov Ballet company. Almost at once the senior ballerina chose him to partner her in a full length ballet and soon he had danced the lead in almost all the big classics.

From then on his career might have been a straightforward success story. But his temperament was too restless and his talent too explosive to fit into a static routine and – worse still – he refused to join a political group, as was expected of all leading dancers. Things came to a head in 1961. At the end of a season by the company in Paris, during which Nureyev's independent behaviour had offended the management, he was threatened with a summary return to Russia. Faced with an instant decision, he broke away from the company at the airport and demanded asylum from the French authorities.

Since that fateful date he has become a world-wide celebrity. After a year with the Marquis de Cuevas company in Paris he made a sensational debut in London at a gala organized by Margot Fonteyn and not long after made his first appearance in New York. Soon he was a permanent guest artist with the Royal Ballet and appearing regularly with Fonteyn to form a partnership which quickly grew into a legend. It was not long before he embarked on the gruelling international round of engagements which was to be his regualr routine, jetting from city to city to fill a schedule which would cripple any normal dancer. Not content with that, he has choreographed and produced ballets for many major companies. He has packed a whole lifetime of dance activities into a few years.

His character seems to have been custom-designed for his career. He has energy, courage, persistance, cunning, intelligence and charm. He is both tough and sensitive, persistent and disconcertingly mercurial. A streak of schoolboy mischief preserves him from pretentiousness but he has a strong sense of professional dignity. Above all he is invincibly self-contained and self-centred. He has always had to stand up for himself and he is a natural fighter. He was born to be an outsider and he has made it a strength. Nothing and nobody comes between himself and his work.

Nureyev has put down no roots. He has no nationality, no fixed attachment to any one dance company and no permanent home – a gipsy status which seems to suit him exactly. He has a house in the hills above Monte Carlo and London has for many year been his base, but most of his time is spent flying from one capital to another. He has probably the biggest first-hand knowledge of international dance and dancers in the world and has friends everywhere.

His normal day begins, as with all dancers, with a gruelling practice class and is filled with endless rehearsals, interviews, telephone calls and business discussions. He makes all his

Nureyev as actor. A dramatic moment as the romantic hero of Kenneth Macmillan's production of *Romeo and Juliet* for the Royal Ballet.

intricate arrangements himself: he keeps no engagement diary but carries six months' schedules in his head. His life-style is as flexible as his temperament. He tends to live in pop star conditions, camping out in luxury hotel rooms. He likes old clothes and shoes, seldom looks in a mirror and is quite happy to go directly from rehearsal to a cinema in his rumpled practice costume.

The thing about him which strikes most people at once is his restless energy. His routine of dance performances is legendary – he fits in four times more than normal – and on top of this he finds time and strength to keep up with films and plays and lead a lively social life. What is more he is a TV addict who can sit before the set all night. He is a bad sleeper, a good listener, an intelligent (but surprisingly indulgent) critic and – when he is in the mood – an amusing talker.

His character has certainly helped to keep him in the headlines but it was his dancing which put him there and it is on his dancing that his fame continues to rest. It is of a kind which occurs only rarely, with a quality which stirs people not otherwise interested in ballet. Several critics have pointed out that the explosion of popularity of dance in recent years can be dated almost precisely from Nureyev's arrival in the West. It is no accident that today it is the male dancers who draw the big crowds, not the ballerinas.

His dancing does not fit comfortably into any neat category, but has created one of its own. It has ingredients of many qualities – virtuosity, expressiveness, dynamism, grace, savagery, elegance, dramatic power, classical line, drollery, sculptural fullness – but the way he combines them springs from his own nature. He has a giant ego and a rich and mysterious personality and he pours them without reservation into his dancing. He is a demon for perfection, yet he will risk everything when he runs on stage. The experts savour the subtleties; for the general public it is the sense of giving everything, of commitment, of danger which rivets them. On top of this he offers the almost physical pleasure of what we call 'beauty of movement' – a sensual quality which can take on overtones of something more mysterious.

It is this gift which is revealed strongly by the camera. It is not through chance that Nureyev is the most photographed dancer of all time. Leslie Caron, star of over twenty films, said after working with him in *Valentino* – a partnership which, to her great regret, did not include a dance number together: 'Rudolf has physical beauty to a degree which is unbelievable. To see him turn his head is something to write about. He can just stand still and it's beautiful. The thing about films is that the inner qualities are emphasised. His charm and kindness and intelligence come through.'

This affinity with the camera is one of the assets which made him a natural choice to impersonate Valentino: Russell could be certain that he would look good in every frame. But this would be an acting role – what qualifications did he have in this

direction? Nureyev is theatrical to his backbone and any form of theatre is as natural to him as breathing. To turn his talent from ballet to the screen did not require one of his great leaps but just one of the supple twists which send shivers down the spines of his fans. The faithless hero in the ballet *Giselle* is a subtle psychological study and roles like Romeo, Hamlet or Othello, the puppet Petrushka or the rebellious and then repenting Prodigal Son – all these parts require expressive acting.

All the same it was a risk to use him for such a huge dramatic role. 'It was a tremendous gamble,' admits Peter Suschitsky, the Director of Photography, 'but Russell seems to take that kind of risk almost subconsciously. Before we started I was full of fear that the central core of the film would be weak. There were imminent elements of a clash – Russell tends to approach people with a will to dominate. But in the end Nureyev transcended them. He decided just to be professional and hardworking, and he was, right through the film.' Russell himself had no doubts. 'He's just right for the part,' he declared, 'I waited for a year until he was free and I've never done that before. He has this unique mystique, magic, charisma, call it what you like. He's perhaps the most glamorous yet mysterious figure in the world today.'

Nureyev, on his side, had few reservations about working with Russell. 'We both have strong personalities and opinions,

Above
Nureyev relaxes with one of the characters from the film.

Opposite above
Valentino (Nureyev) and his co-star Lorna (Penelope Milford) in a scene from the *Monsieur Beaucaire* **sequence.**

Opposite below
Nureyev in his *Monsieur Beaucaire* **costume receives some last minute attentions from his dresser.**

but it was his film, and naturally he knows far more about films than I do. I had seen several of his television films, 'Isadora' and 'Debussy' which I liked very much; and I had really enjoyed his feature films, especially *Women in Love* and *The Music Lovers;* that was an amazing picture of an extraordinary man and his circle. And I thought *Tommy* was fantastic as a record of a certain period, the age of rock-opera. What I admire about his work is that it always has a positive angle, a strong point of view.

'Some time ago the question of our doing a film about Nijinsky together came up, but it fell through owing to difficulties on both sides. Then, later, he asked me to impersonate the dancer as a small role in his new film on Valentino. I said I would, and then a few days afterwards he rang up and said that he'd been thinking about the whole thing and that he would like me to play the leading part – Valentino himself. I thought it over for a few days and then said, "Yes, why not?" It wasn't the first time I had been offered the part. De Sica had suggested it to me some years ago.'

Nureyev already knew quite a lot about Valentino. 'He's very well-known in Russia, just as much as in the West. I got my first sharp impression of him during my very first big dancing role in Leningrad. I was dancing in a ballet called *Laurencia* with the top ballerina Natalia Dudinskaya, when I saw a piece of Valentino film – *Blood and Sand,* I think it was. In

Above
Nureyev and Michelle Phillips face the cameras for a seaside shot.

Opposite
Convincingly bruised and battered – Nureyev as Valentino after his victory in the boxing ring.

On pages 24-25
Nureyev as Valentino in one of his earliest film roles – a slapstick comedy – before his real talents were spotted.

it there's a scene which shows the cruelty of the public towards him. Afterwards I told Dudinskaya how horrible and frightening I thought that would be and how some people did not seem to understand it. She replied, "Well, what about us dancers? People out there are just waiting for us to fall down and break a leg, to get a taste of blood." That was the first time I thought about Valentino.

'Then much later, after I had come to the West, I was given a compilation film on Valentino by Universal Pictures. It was a two-reeler which shows his life and some shots from his films. It starts with his funeral and works backwards, just as Russell's does – I don't know if he had seen it when his script was being written.

'I was very impressed by Valentino's acting. In those days film actors were very jittery. Valentino was much slower, more sinuous in his movements. He would hold still and just turn his head or move his hand to indicate an emotion. At that time I didn't know he had done ballroom dancing, but there is a dance quality in his movement. With him it was natural; I don't know that he would have made a real dancer. In the sequences where he does actually dance, the way he does the steps is rather awkward – but maybe they were badly edited. His basic postures are remarkable.

'It wasn't his looks which counted but his acting. He had a certain conviction, and that's the prime thing about acting – to be able to believe at short notice in what you're doing. If you're not convinced inside you it will not look right, either on the

Above
Nureyev portrays the desperation of Valentino as he tries to escape the taunts of fellow inmates in prison.

Opposite
Nureyev in one of the suits made for him by Valentino's Savile Row tailors, based on an original pattern.

screen or in the theatre.' Leslie Caron made the same point after Russell had shown her some films of Valentino. 'I was amazed at what a good actor he was – not only good, remarkable. Very still, with lots of inner thinking, which is what you can do in a film; he knew what the camera can do. He was a handsome man, but you realize that his tremendous fame was due not to his looks but to his performance. He was completely dedicated to each part, from the make-up to the gestures, the costumes, the walk, the stance – everything was studied.'

Nureyev's first task, once he had agreed to do the film – a major commitment, since it would cut five months out of the schedule of a man who had never before gone more than three weeks without dancing – was to study the script attentively to form his conception of the role. 'When I first read the screenplay, Valentino's character seemed to me rather unsympathetic. He let himself be pushed around by everybody and took insults from his critics without answering back. I felt personally about that, about his need to fight for himself. However dumb one is, sooner or later one's self-preservation machine begins to work. I thought I would make him more positive, less passive. For instance he must have had a really strong love for Rambova to take so much from her.

'As a man he seems to have been completely confused. He

Above
Nureyev poses as Valentino at home in his Hollywood mansion.

was in a predicament. He found himself in a situation with which neither he nor anybody else could cope. That's how success works. Everybody becomes jealous and possessive and demanding and, when they don't get what they ask for, they start to tear you to pieces. That remark of Dudinskaya wasn't true just of his time. It is a reality always.

'Valentino seems to have been rather a gentle character. He lived surrounded by men, though that doesn't necessarily mean anything; there's an Italian life-style in which the men always stick together quite normally. I don't think he was very active sexually.

'When you remember that in Valentino's time there was no TV so that the cinema was the only form of mass-media, you realize what disproportionate emotions a film star of his magnitude must have aroused and how much play the press must have made with him – much more than they would today. Every move he made must have fascinated the public. That process of familiarization must have been incredible and so the pressure on him would be much harder. He became so much caught up with it and with the code of honour and so on, that the "powder puff" attack really affected him. I can understand. I know how I react when some nonsense is written about me. And he too lived and worked in a foreign environment. He wasn't a house product, and that is always upsetting to the aboriginal artists.'

Opposite
Final preparations for Nureyev as Valentino in the role of soldier in *The Four Horsemen of the Apocalypse.*

30

The affinities between the new star and the old became clear to everybody concerned with the film, but there were still doubts about whether Nureyev would be able to translate them onto the screen. The atmosphere when he arrived in Spain to begin shooting was tense. All the rest of the team, with an assortment of wives and children, were already waiting in Almeria, a resort on the extreme southernmost coast of Spain which has become a kind of miniature Hollywood. Nureyev flew in direct from New York, the day after a triumphant farewell performance, at the Metropolitan Opera House, of his own production of Tchaikovsky's *The Sleeping Beauty* during which he had received a standing ovation in the middle of the ballet after a sensational solo. 'We just didn't know what would happen. Everyone was terrified of his first spoken line,' recalled the designer Philip Harrison later.

Nureyev rides out to film a scene as the Sheik.

His first assignment, the morning after he arrived, was with Gillian Gregory, the choreographer who was to be responsible for the dances in the film, to learn the 'gaucho tango'. Gregory (who had worked with Russell on *The Boy Friend*) was apprehensive when they met in a hotel foyer: 'I can only equate my nervousness with my feelings when I did a number in the Royal Command Performance. These were my two worst moments ever. I asked Nureyev if he wanted to do some basic tango steps first, but he said "No." So I said "OK" and then I looked at his feet. He'd got enormous boots on. "What's the matter?" he asked. "Well, those aren't really the right shoes for tangoing in." He just said, "I like to wear them," and I thought "Oh God!" Actually he had a point – it was one of those stone Spanish floors, but they really were awful. He wasn't exactly difficult, he just didn't give in at all.'

Another fraught moment followed, when Nureyev had to submit to having his long mane of hair – one of his personal trademarks – trimmed down. The style of the Valentino period was 'short back and sides'. Russell wanted a really close cut; Nureyev, suffering no doubt from a touch of the Samson complex and also from nervousness about the effect on his appearance, wished for a compromise. In the end Russell won – more or less. Nureyev emerged from the exhausted hairdresser with a new look. Sharp eyes will notice a slight difference in length between the desert and the later scenes.

In the afternoon was the bullfight sequence, with script rehearsals in the hotel in the evening. Next day was to be Nureyev's first spoken line, a nerve-racking moment of truth. 'I had the same experience when I started, in *An American in Paris,*' said Leslie Caron. 'It's doubly difficult for a dancer to speak. You're used to expressing yourself silently ,'suddenly you have to break through the inhibition barrier. In my case I had to yell at Gene Kelly across the whole set, "Gerry, I love you!" It was horrendous – worse than performing some sex act in front of a crowd.' Caron noticed that Nureyev's voice was pitched higher than usual on that first day, from nervousness; but he managed his lines successfully. 'Afterwards everybody

Nureyev enjoys a joke on the set.

congratulated me,' said Marcella Markham, the American actress who had been allotted the task of transforming his Russian accent into Italian-American. 'I think they should have congraulated him!' She had had much acting experience herself in New York and London and had been dialogue coach for many productions including some for the National Theatre. She and Nureyev worked together for long hours to arrive at the mixture of Brooklyn and Italy which was Valentino's speaking voice. 'The trouble is that Nureyev has a very musical ear,' she remarked afterwards. 'He would get it right very quickly, but by the twentieth take he had been listening to English accents and he would unconsciously revert to them.' The film convention is that all suggestions to the actors have to be made through the director. Afraid of interrupting Russell's concentration, she set up a communication system with Nureyev during shooting which involved sending messages via the make-up expert or the dresser who whispered reminders while mopping up perspiration or repairing a broken button.

Nureyev quickly relaxed – too much so on one occasion. The first scene he was involved in was the shooting of *The Four Horsemen of the Apocalypse.* In it a car drives up and Leslie Caron, in the character of Nazimova, looks round imperiously and demands: 'Which is he, the Italian boy whose name wafts like garlic from every breath in town?' 'She was so funny,' says Nureyev, 'that I just burst out laughing and spoilt the take. She gave her whole part so much vitality. She put a touch of vulgarity into it which gave it a kind of inner lustre. It was really great to work with her.'

Nureyev waits for the cameras to roll for the boxing sequence.

Conditions for these first shots were pretty tough. The heat was intense; the horse on which Nureyev had to pose for a 'dream vision' as the abducting Sheik proved uncooperative ('Every time I gazed into the distance it flopped its ears'); and violent gusts of wind blew up which, while eagerly seized on by the camera-man, blew sand into everything. Nureyev became impatient and, tired of standing around while a scene was being filmed on the beach, he walked into the sea for a dip – nearly spoiling the next shot by swimming into the picture.

As a matter of fact Nureyev was by no means a newcomer to filming. 'My first appearance before the camera was when I was six years old. A news team came to my kindergarten to photograph us dancing. Of course I was terribly anxious to see myself on the screen; but when the shot appeared I had been cut out. I expect I didn't look enough like a typical Tartar; I was a blond boy and most Tartars are dark.

'But my real film debut was when they recorded a *pas de deux* after it had won a prize in a student competition in Moscow. I was very interested to see it. I was curious to find out why the public got so excited about my dancing. I must say I was rather disappointed, but I was fascinated by the whole process.' After he came to the West he appeared in several dance films: *An Evening with the Royal Ballet, Romeo and Juliet,* his own productions of *Swan Lake* and *Don Quixote* – which he also directed – and a film about his work, *I am a Dancer.*

'I learnt a lot by watching them and my ballet experience naturally helped me in this film; after all ballet is a theatre art, it's a form of acting. Acting in an opera house isn't so different from acting before a camera. The speed and the scale don't matter, in both cases the essential thing is that it has to be carried to completion – and on stage you can't lie.

'I think Russell's dance background shows in his direction – not in a direct way, but in the way every scene is composed. It's not exactly a dance composition but something of the same kind. In fact he could probably direct a ballet quite easily. He often seems to put dancing into his films, but in this one he actually took some out. There was originally to have been an

Nureyev as Valentino faces his opponent in the boxing arena.

extract from *Petrushka,* with me watching from a box and being beaten up as the puppet is in the ballet – a bit of heavy symbolism – and also a sort of Busby Berkeley number. And he cut a fantasy dance I did with Felicity Kendal and a dance number for Leslie Caron and also some of Michelle Phillips' dancing.

'He uses a videotape playback machine in which you can see at once what you have achieved and what you have missed. That didn't frighten me at all – I like to know exactly where I'm succeeding or failing, in fact I insisted on seeing every take. I would certainly use it again if I could, if I make another film. Russell wrote his own script as I believe he often does. The dialogue could be improved, I suppose, but the mechanics – the ideas and the imagination – are fascinating. He is always especially interested in the placing of the shot in its background, either going along with it or contrasting the action against it. I had been told he was difficult to work with, but I didn't find him so. I found him very considerate. He discusses things all the time and he listens and in general he's a very open person. He's generous and vital artistically and he's vulnerable in a quite overt way. He's like a gigantic clam. He opens.

himself to everybody and then when he gets hurt that huge shell of his shuts with a bang. On those occasions Bob Chartoff was a great help. He's a natural pacifier, a catalyst. He not only brought things to a boil but now and then he took them off. Of course Russell shouts at people sometimes, but no more than we shout at ballet rehearsals. To me all that was nothing. It's just that film actors are not exposed enough to the rough and tumble of work. I found this filming a thousand times easier than dancing. I think dancers are saints – dancing is such an incredible strain, both physically and mentally. Russell likes to do lots of takes – sometimes up to twenty – but I didn't mind that at all. After all, in ballet you do your own retakes constantly in front of the mirror: to do things many times is a routine for me, I feel comfortable in the system. Film actors don't seem to have to work as hard as ballet people and theatre people.'

In fact Nureyev always found time to do his ballet classes as well as filming. On location he would do them during the lunch hour. From the Elstree studio he would drive direct into London and put in two hours' practice at night. He would film from 8 am to 7 pm. and at 7.30 he was at the barre. On top of

Nureyev in practice costume doing his daily ballet exercises on one of the sets during an interval on the filming.

During one of the many periods of waiting,
Nureyev passes the time by reading a
newspaper.

this he was choreographing his *Romeo and Juliet* with dancers
from the London Festival Ballet and also learning a new role
(Glen Tetley's *Pierrot Lunaire*). He also did about eight performances with the Royal Ballet at Covent Garden while still
shooting. He would go straight from the set to the theatre.
One day, his hair had been curled for a scene in the film as the
'all-American boy' and he had no time to uncurl it. Some of the
audience were alarmed at what they thought was his new
hairstyle. His industry recalls the routines of Valentino, who
used to get up at 7 am to take lessons in riding and fencing. 'He
imposed a certain discipline on himself,' says Nureyev, 'while
some modern actors don't.' This kind of comment betrays the
strains which the drawn-out rhythms of filming were impos-
ing on a naturally impatient character accustomed to a much
more concentrated routine. The tension involved in the
exceptionally long shooting schedule was foreseeable; but
Nureyev too is armed with a fierce self-control. The atmosphere on the set might become fraught: 'Russell and Nureyev
both behaved very professionally but they didn't get close;
Russell was never comfortable with him,' commented
Jonathan Benson the Assistant Director. But he never swerved
from the job and never uttered a word of complaint outside the
studio. He was committed as few people know how; he had
put himself without reserve in the hands of a director he
admired and respected, Ken Russell.

THE RUSSELL TREATMENT

For most film-goers the name Ken Russell provokes mixed and violent reactions. Inspiring reverence in some quarters, consternation in others, he is a figure impossible to overlook or feel neutral about. Today he is the best-known – and also the most controversial – of British directors. To date he has made ten feature films – most of which have proved commercially successful. All have had their admirers, most have raised opposition. He is the *enfant terrible* of the British cinema, steadfastly refusing to subscribe to the national belief in discretion, restraint and so-called good taste, which he considers a euphemism for cold feet. His 'appalling talent', as the London critic Dilys Powell described it in a memorable phrase, is unconventional and unique.

Like many an artistic outsider, he springs from the most normal of backgrounds. The son of a modest businessman, he was born in 1927 in Southampton, a large seaport in the south of England. He seems to have had a dreamy, self-absorbed childhood. His memories are of the rather run-down beauty spots of the neighbouring countryside, the crumbling cliffs, bungalows and stony beaches. A nostalgia for his childhood can be detected beneath the surface of many of his rebellious gestures. In *Valentino* he actually used a house in a resort a few miles from his birthplace for the star's Hollywood home; while a picnic sequence scheduled to be shot in one of his favourite areas in the New Forest was only abandoned after torrential rain had washed away the film unit for three days in succession. When he was eight years old he was given a 9.5 mm projector for Christmas and at once embarked on what was to be his great obsession. His first home movies included Felix the Cat, Betty Boob and Mickey Mouse cartoons, and Charlie Chaplin and Harold Lloyd one-reel comedies. From

Russell directs Nureyev and Penelope Milford in the love scene in the *Monsieur Beaucaire* sequence.

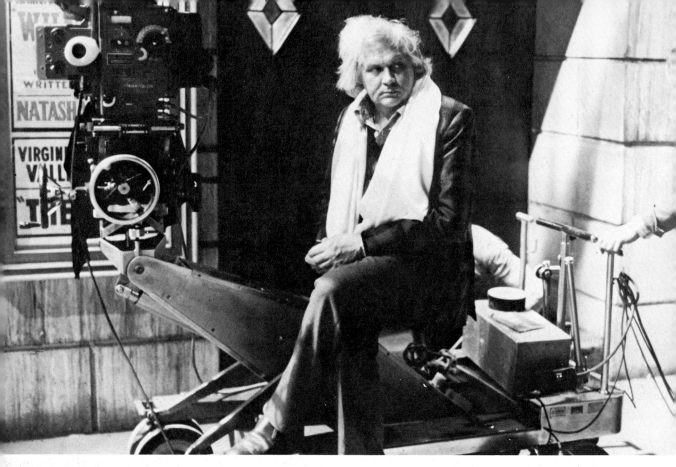

Russell on the set.

these he graduated to the full splendour of a 35 mm Butcher projector, salvaged off the old transatlantic liner *Mauretania* which was being broken up in the local shipyards. He got it for £10, together with a trunkful of silent films.

They were a strange mixture but magical to a child's eye and he seems never to have forgotten the hand-tinted travel scenes and naïve thrills of those early dramas. But 35 mm films were scarce so he returned to his 9.5 projector and found an old chemist's shop from which he could hire films by people like Fritz Lang and Leni Riefenstahl. He acquired a taste for Expressionism. During the war years *Metropolis* and *Siegfried* used to flicker on a makeshift screen in the garage to the sound of a record of Arthur Bliss's march from the film *Things to Come*. The music was often drowned by the noise of sirens and falling bombs which emptied the improvised theatre instantly. 'The audience never stopped to ask for a refund, either through fright, or because the proceeds were donated to the Spitfire Fund,' said Russell.

His progress toward his future career as a film maker was, however, to prove erratic. He attended a nautical school (where he made his first short film), trained as an Air Force electrician (when he became a passionate music lover) and – inspired by an extraordinary ex-dancer sailor – he tried to break into the world of ballet and the theatre. This attempt was a failure, but success came when he took a course in photography. He soon began to sell his pictures to magazines. He married a fellow-student, was converted to Catholicism and made two short films with the help of a Catholic Institute, *Amelia and the Angel* and *Lourdes*.

His luck changed when he took them to the BBC and showed them to Huw Wheldon, director of the new arts programme *Monitor*. Wheldon liked them and engaged him (to replace John Schlesinger); he stayed with the BBC for ten years, making thirty-four films. The final one, *The Dance of the Seven Veils* (1970) caused such an outcry that the viewing public was split down the middle in violent controversy and questions were raised in Parliament. Russell has not worked for television since. But as far back as 1963 he had already tried his hand at a full length feature film, *French Dressing;* since then he has become one of the few directors whose name is familiar even to a non-film-going public.

His career had begun mildly. His first film for the BBC, *Poet's London* was a nostalgic ramble through the capital and he followed it with a variety of subjects ranging from brass bands to painters. His big breakthrough came with *Elgar* (1962), a gentle study of the composer set in the soft English countryside. Some mildly playful exercises on less serious themes did not dent the image of a sensitive young man with a quiet, conventional future before him.

Then things began to change. *The Debussy Film* (1966)

Director and star discuss a problem.

disconcerted even Huw Wheldon by its violent contrast between the man and his art, and more shocks were to follow. *Isadora Duncan* (1966) presented not a sepia-tinted memento, but what an admiring critic has described as 'a jumble of decadence, beauty and vulgarity', a striking vision which broke decisively out of the expected style and took the critics by surprise.

He reverted to a quieter mood in *Song of Summer* (1968), an ironic but beautifully controlled impression of Delius, a composer who put his dreams into his music and his aggressions into his life. This was followed in the next year by a feature film which won almost universal praise. *Women in Love,* adapted from the novel by D. H. Lawrence. His reputation as an important director was established.

But his next (and last) work for the BBC sent a tremor through the nerves of lovers of propriety and bourgeois sensibility. In *The Dance of the Seven Veils* he took a composer whom he positively disliked, Richard Strauss, and flayed what he regarded as his betrayal of his ideals in a succession of extravagant and deliberately farcical images. Anti-German overtones were suspected and internationalists and admirers of the composer were deeply offended. The vigour, not to say violence, of his attack alarmed the guardians of good taste; they were even more shocked by Russell's feature film on Tchaikovsky released soon after. The ironic treatment and exaggerated visual metaphors in *The Music Lovers* proved too strong for most conventional film critics and pained admirers of the composer; but the public flocked to see it and many of the images have passed into film legend.

Russell as actor; he plays Rex Ingram who directed Valentino in his first major film, *The Four Horsemen of the Apocalypse.*

The star and the director. Nureyev's hair is smoothed into the proper Valentino style under Russell's critical eye.

His subsequent films – *The Devils* (1971), *Savage Messiah* (1972), *Mahler* (1974), *Tommy* (1975), *Lisztomania* (1975) – confirmed his mature style and easily recognisable tone of voice. They have the unmistakable stamp of a private creative mind; their strength and weaknesses are inextricable, being the two sides of a single, strong personality.

Russell is a stocky man with a shock of wild greying hair, a taste for flamboyant clothes and a quiet manner concealing a furious charge of energy. *Valentino* meant keeping up enthusiasm and concentration for a period of nearly a year and a half – during the preparation of the script, the casting, the long shooting schedule and the editing. He has been actively concerned with the production side of many of his films and written most of his own scripts. He is a family man with a wife and five children (four boys and one girl). His wife Shirley designs the costumes for his films, discusses their progress every evening and also runs a costume hire business called 'The Last Picture Frock'. The children are often called in to play parts ranging from crowd work to featured roles.

'What I like about Russell,' says Leslie Caron, 'is that he keeps a sort of home-movie feeling in his work, as though it was a cottage industry. He and his wife go on working as though they were still in their own backyard.' This home-made flavour runs through many of his films, giving them a

Russell watches attentively as Valentino (Nureyev) dances with one of the older customers (Mildred Shay) at the tea-room where he is employed as a professional dancer.

free-wheeling improvisatory freedom despite their dependence on big set-pieces. Russell is not interested in the world of movie people other than his own and he makes no attempt to keep up with the latest trendy developments in the cinema. He has managed to preserve a childlike wonder and imagination and independence of mind. 'One of the things I like about films,' he has written, 'is the Odyssey factor. There's the excitement of setting out on a journey. You don't know what is going to happen. You have good adventures and bad adventures. People get killed on the way. But you experience a lot of excitement and it's the moments when something unexpected and fantastic happens that make it all worthwhile.'

This readiness to improvise, to snatch at chance ideas or unplanned opportunities, is a basic part of his approach. He gives his actors immense freedom to change their roles or introduce their own interpretations. 'I was amazed at first,' says Gillian Gregory, who arranged the dances in *Valentino*. 'I was a bit frightened too, because that also leaves you room to make mistakes. I see now that he just takes what he likes from your ideas and restructures them – so if you use your freedom sensibly, you're all right.'

This easy-going approach may be frightening to inexperienced performers but it is welcomed by old hands, particularly those trained in the improvisatory American style. 'Russell is extremely creative,' says Michelle Phillips. 'He inspires you. You aren't locked up in the dialogue or the script, he's always willing to talk about it.' 'He's a genius – I'd put him beside William Wyler,' said the veteran actor Huntz Hall, who plays Lasky in *Valentino* and was one of the original Dead End Kids. 'It's a pity England hasn't got a few more Ken Russells.' But sometimes his confiding approach causes disappointment. Actors and technicians who have felt they had become indispensible suddenly find they are not; Russell retains a personal control in all departments, from costumes to lighting. 'He really just uses you to bounce off,' adds Gregory wryly.

Many of his actors get the impression that he is not much interested in details of acting. 'If Ken Russell has a fault, it is that he is not forceful with the actors,' says Seymour Cassell. Russell is the first to admit this bias. 'I don't know how to direct actors,' he has written. 'I can talk to them and tell them what I think it's all about but I can't make them act and I'm not interested in doing so. That's up to them. What I can do is choose people and create a working environment in which they can breathe and expand.'

'People who work with him walk about as if slightly bemused' said his assistant director Jonathan Benson. He does not become intimate with the actors or crew he is working with, though he likes to keep up a cheerful relaxed atmosphere. He works intuitively and sometimes relays music on to the set while shooting to set up a mood and rhythm, just as the silent-movie directors did in the past. 'Many of my best effects are achieved with the use of music, which is why I am sometimes admired more by musicians than by many of the film purists of today who seem to deny the true nature of the cinema,' he claims.

It seems generally agreed that Russell is above all a visual director. Perhaps he is still haunted by the silent images which flickered in the garage in Southampton, the slapstick acrobatics, emphatic acting and fantastic hand-tinted sets. 'I am eaten up by the image, with the way things look,' he admits himself. Wheldon spotted this characteristic early on. 'Words were tricky for him,' he has said of Russell's BBC days. 'He used them rhetorically, abrasively, irrationally. His strength lies in the imagination, in the leap of the mind's eye.'

'If the word genius is applicable to any contemporary artists, I think history will prove that Russell is one of the few in the film world today,' declares Chartoff. 'He has a really extraordinary gift for finding images which express emotion in a way which transcends words or actions. He puts his thoughts and feelings on celluloid as a painter puts them on a canvas. It's an instinct – an instinct backed by incredibly hard work.'

It is these far-flying visual metaphors which have become the hallmark of a Russell film. The use of extravagant fantasy is not unique in the film world ('I call him the Fellini of the North,' remarked Leslie Caron); but Russell deliberately uses a kind of billboard exaggeration as a way of puncturing myth and reaching truth. He often combines elements from two kinds of film he loved as a schoolboy – the German Expressionist

Russell and his assistant director Jonathan Benson, watch a playback on the videotape machine with Alfred Marks who plays Richard Rowland.

dramas and the early Hollywood slapstick movies. To this blend he adds his own brand of ferocious irony. It is a disturbing mixture, and one especially alarming to sticklers for aesthetic refinement. 'It's strange that people can't reconcile vulgarity with artistry,' says Russell. 'They're the same thing to me . . . By vulgarity I mean an exuberant over-the-top, larger-than-life, slightly bad taste, red-blooded, but essentially human thing. If that's nothing to do with art, let's have nothing to do with art.' Shakespeare himself would have agreed with him.

The subjects picked on for the Russell treatment have often been drawn from the world of entertainment. The choice has obviously been partly based on his own early enthusiasms – music, dance and the theatre. But he may also have favoured it because he has found in the lives of performers the most vivid symbols of his favourite subject – the conflict between fantasy and reality. In this battle – although it sometimes needs a keen eye to determine his allegiance – Russell is totally on the side of reality and artistic purity. Behind the savage buffoon lies a romantic idealist, a Don Quixote disguised as Sancho Panza who charges giants and windmills with dedicated and joyful ferocity.

It seems inevitable that one day Rudolph Valentino would drop into focus in the Russell lens. His story combined all the

Beside one of the period props — the figurine of a camel – Russell and Marcella Markham, Nureyev's voice coach, discuss a point in the script with Nureyev.

ingredients which fire Russell's imagination – public glamour, private suffering, the clash between commercial greed and simple, personal ideals, the whole amalgam magnified to spectacular proportions. Valentino's story often reads like a Russell script. and the character himself seemed destined to become the axle-pin of a whirling, dazzling Russell firework.

The film did not develop in that way. While still unmistakeably a Ken Russell picture, with vertiginous switches from comedy to tragedy, from real to blown-up emotions, *Valentino* has no balloon flights into fantasy land. There has been no need to underline or exaggerate because the truth was already outsize, over-written. Russell has been able to play it practically straight.

The result is a film consistent in style and mood. The hysteria is contained within the script. The big set pieces – the Fatty commotion, the *Four Horsemen* sequence, the boxing match, the mortuary dramatics – fall into place naturally because they are biographically believable. The prison scene is magnified but not distorted. Only in isolated sequences – Lasky communicating with an ape, a powder-puff cabaret, couples fox-trotting round the boxing ring – has Russell let his fancy off the lead. Apart from a quite conventional use of flashback there is hardly a cinematic trick in the whole film, which is shot in real, or at least realistic, settings and authentic period costumes, shot with unpretentious but elegant camera

Nureyev listens to Russell as the final touches are given to his make-up for *Monsieur Beaucaire*.

Russell explains his ideas about a scene from
Monsieur Beaucaire.

work. Russell has never lost sight of the human story.

In compiling his screenplay – which, like most scripts, went through several versions – Russell has used his usual techniques. He zooms in on a few incidents and expands them to produce the maximum effect. Many of his visions seem to have been sparked off by still photographs of the period. His Valentino makes spaghetti much in the style of a genuine shot of the screen hero; the Nijinsky tango recalls an old photograph of a demonstration by Valentino in front of a gramophone; the half-naked love-scene in the *Monsieur Beaucaire* wig echoes a dressing-room sequence in the original film. He seems to have encapsulated a number of the real-life incidents into his screenplay. The prison scene combines the discomforts of a cell in California with the probably more horrific night which the young Valentino spent in the notorious Tombs prison in New York. Russell has taken liberties; but he has not strayed into licence.

His problem was to enclose a many-layered, multi-faceted story within a simple framework. He had to show Valentino as the victim of a commercial society, Valentino as a symbol of innocence blighted by success, Valentino as a fly caught in the monstrous but glittering web of show business, Valentino as the supreme sex symbol. He was all that, but he was also a human individual. That dilemma is what Russell's film is all about.

SHOOTING THE STARS

Shooting for *Valentino* began in August in Almeria in Spain and ended twenty-one weeks later in No. 2 studio at the EMI 'Elstree' studios at Borehamwood in England. During all this time responsibility for the practical side of the operation rested on the British Associate Producer, Harry Benn, who had already discussed the script in Los Angeles and had drawn up the budget and proposed schedules. Everything, from the hire of the studios to providing toilets and period headgear, came under his experienced eye (he had worked with Russell several times already). It was he who chartered the plane which carried the directors, the actors, the ninety other people and a load of 'sensitive equipment' to Spain one Sunday.

The site chosen for the first shots – scenes from the *Four Horsemen* and *The Sheik* episodes – was a stretch of sand about twenty miles inland called 'The Dunes'. Here Harrison had set up trenches and barbed wire for one scene and a tent and some palm trees for the other. Several 60 foot palms had been brought 200 miles from Alicante and buried in concrete so that they should not blow over – a wise precaution as a sudden but picturesque hurricane sprang up during the shooting.

From Almeria the whole outfit, now numbering 130, flew up to Barcelona for a dramatic one day's date in the zoo. Russell had heard of a rare white gorilla there, and was bent on using it. The whole gorilla house was turned into a set, where Huntz Hall and 'Snowball' glowered at each other through the bars. 'An expensive luxury' remarked Benn; and a joke went round that Snowball was the highest paid star in the picture.

From Barcelona the party proceeded to S'Agaro on the Costa Brava for some beach shots, and thence to England where most of the shooting was

Nureyev as the Sheik — the role which established Valentino irrevocably as the screen's Great Lover – with Jennie Linden as Agnes Ayres.

Philip Harrison
1976

done in the Elstree studio. It forms part of a large drab group of buildings standing behind a wire fence at the end of a provincial high street lined with shops. The huge windowless studios huddle together like factory buildings, surrounded by prefabricated huts for the various special services – props, costumes, stunt equipment, cutting (*Valentino* was edited in a tiny room about 12 foot square, with Russell and Stuart Baird, the editor, crouched together among ribbons of film). In front of them is a low brick building for offices; the passages are so long that it feels like walking inside a zeppelin. Chartoff's room was upstairs overlooking a bank, a snack-bar, and the Red Lion pub. Downstairs muffled dialogue comes from a viewing theatre; a lady sits at a desk in front of a cut out poster of Valentino in an embrace.

Entering the studio is like walking into a railway station at night. It is enormously high and dark, with huge hooks and chains (for moving sets) hanging from the roof, half-made scenery standing about and cables twisting across the floor like snakes. At the far end a brilliant light illuminates a corner against which dark figures sit or stand motionlessly. An overpowering smell of incense smoke fills the air. The chiaroscuro is as dramatic as in a Rembrandt engraving. You

Design by Philip Harrison for the funeral parlor set.

52

The opulent funeral parlor set in which Valentino's body lies in state.

can make out Russell vivid in a red sweater with his mane of grey hair, and Chartoff in a duffle jacket. There are tables piled with papers and handbags and paper cups everywhere. A trolley stands by with coffee and chocolate biscuits (Nureyev has his own bag of Chelsea buns). There are over thirty people on the twilit set. One of the crew sits reading *The Guardian*. A mink coat lies across a typewriter. The dialogue coach is knitting a long red stocking.

'Quiet everybody, please,' shouts Jonathan Benson. Suddenly there is complete silence. 'Can we have some more cigar smoke? Standby! Ready! OK – action!' A tough young man with blondish curly hair walks briskly into the lights in plus-fours, smoking a pipe. 'Howdy, ma'am?' he asks. The accent is Texan but the voice is unmistakably that of Nureyev, playing an all-American boy. He begins to cough, unused to smoking. Felicity Kendal makes her pseudo-telephone-call for the twelfth time. Half a minute of *Valentino* is 'in the can'.

The speed with which the shells of whole rooms or streets are assembled and dismantled takes ones breath away. Everything had been worked out months before by Philip Harrison, though subject to last minute changes when Russell finally saw it. The funeral parlor was a special problem. 'The obvious idea

Michelle Phillips and Leslie Caron in costumes designed by Shirley Russell.

was a lot of wreaths, but I had made it very architectural. At first we tried a few flowers and Russell asked me what I thought of them. "Actually, I hate them," I said. "I hate them too; let's get them out." Then two days later, he suddenly suggested: "Let's try filling it up with flowers completely!" And that turned out right.'

Such last minute alterations meant changes for everybody. Shirley Russell had begun her 300 costume designs a year before, but in the new funeral parlor set her gown for Leslie Caron looked wrong. It was abandoned, but by good luck she found a genuine period one the day before shooting (nearly half of Michelle Phillips' costumes were originals). But she kept the train with its hundreds of hand-sewn camelias, which brought another anxious look into Harry Benn's eye.

Nureyev's matador costúme was made by Maestra Nesti who outfits Spain's best bullfighters, and his four suits were authentic, specially made by Savile Row tailors, Anderson and Shepherd. They had made suits for Valentino and still had his measurements – he had a 38 inch chest, a 32 inch waist and – surprisingly – was nearly 6 feet tall. Nureyev is shorter,

Opposite
Designs by Shirley Russell for two of the costumes worn by Rambova and Nazimova.

"Valentino"

hard edge
black
cloche.

"4 Horsemen
of the
Apocalypse"
Set.

Michelle
Phillips.
Two piece dress
in "Shell-shock"
panne velvet
chiffon.

Leslie Caron -
Black sleeveless
Riding habit
made from
embroidered
Tablecover.
Blue lingerie satin
Shirt.
Black boots e
Panama.

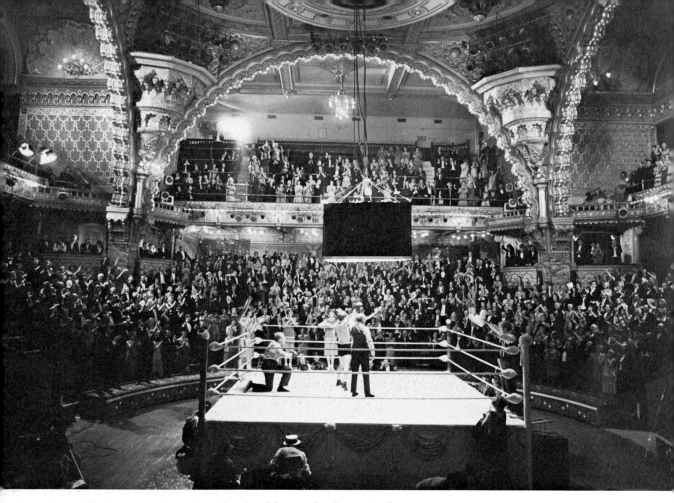

The Circus ring inside the Blackpool Tower makes an impressive setting for the boxing sequence.

but with the same chest, broader shoulders and a dramatically slimmer waist, only 29 inches. He alarmed the tailors by allowing them only one trial fitting. But having made suits for Fred Astaire they knew that the fit must be snug, though with extra room round the arm-holes for a dancer's freedom of movement.

The lighting of Harrison's sets and Shirley Russell's costumes – a vital element of the finished picture – was the responsibility of the Director of Photography, Peter Suschitsky, who had worked with Russell on *Lisztomania*. 'Russell's very visual approach is a great help' he said, 'but he can be demanding. He has strong obsessions which are sometimes difficult to understand. He has an obsessive fear of things being cut off, for instance, and will do retakes just to get a fraction of an inch more headroom or space round the feet, retakes not for an improved performance but for the camera. He gets interested in small details. I wanted to try some misty period camera work, but he likes everything sharp. I tried to match Russell's style as much as I could, by not shying away from being bold and operatic.'

Controlling the whole crowd of actors and crew on the set was Jonathan Benson, whose biggest tests came when the film was being shot on location – in a vintage museum in Bournemouth (which stayed open to mystified visitors throughout the

A lavish ballroom in the Blackpool Tower is filled with crowds watching Valentino and Rambova give their demonstration dance to advertise a cosmetics firm.

Peter Suschitsky, the Director of Photography.

shooting), and above all in the Circus ring and the immense ballroom (only the second biggest) in Blackpool Tower. This weird 500 foot imitation of the Eiffel Tower, built in 1894 on the edge of the sea at a resort in north-west England – a site suggested by Harrison, who had played the saxophone there when touring in his youth with a pop group – posed problems for Harry Benn. It had to be booked months before and there was not enough room for the wardrobe and makeup for the crowd who watched the boxing match (600 haircuts by 12 hairdressers, about 1000 costumes and two restaurants for lunch). In the Circus the local extras in their evening clothes shouted themselves hoarse for six days watching Nureyev slogging away at an amiable British actor, Peter Vaughan. Nureyev's boxing coach was a stunt man specially flown in from Los Angeles, where he had been working on *Rocky*. 'He was a kind of spin-off,' explained Winkler, who had come over from looking after that film to watch the shooting in Blackpool. 'A marvellous place. I was especially impressed by Russell's involvement in all those scenes.'

There were other picturesque locations – the ballroom of a railway station hotel (for the Nijinsky tango, when Anthony Dowell, as Nijinsky, met Russell for the first time on the dance floor), a sham 'Western' town built in the middle of a Spanish valley, and the bar of a London hotel originally built by King

Edward VII for his mistress Lily Langtry. The spectacle there revealed how thin the borderline is between reality and Russell's fantasy. While Nureyev-Valentino swayed and staggered in a drinking contest to the cheers of a crowd in 1920 costume, queues of genuine tourists were fighting past to get to their rooms, especially to the Langtry boudoir with its L-shaped marble bath, while a salesman fluttered around distributing advertisements for leather goods to everybody.

Through the tangle of actors, onlookers, travellers, equipment, and foreign luggage the figure of Ken Russell weaved like a retriever hunting in the undergrowth – calm but tense, giving off an air of excited awareness of what he was after. There was no hint of the authoritarian or fanatic. 'He's very flexible as a director,' remarked Nureyev, 'He guides, rather than imposes. He will say "Think of this as you speak", or "Valentino would have been thinking of that". He explains a scene and then lets you find out your own way of doing it, your own mechanics.' Jonathan Benson, who knows Russell well, having worked with him ever since *Women in Love*, explains: 'Russell is not such a soloist as many people imagine. He imposes his wavelength on the people who are working with him and then taps their ideas.'

Nureyev, dressed as the Sheik, protects his eyes from the sandstorms between 'takes'.

The freedom he gives his actors leaves room for different attitudes towards the business of film-making to become apparent. There is the highly finished, fiercely committed style of which the ballet-trained Nureyev was a pure example. 'During the filming I discovered that there are two kinds of

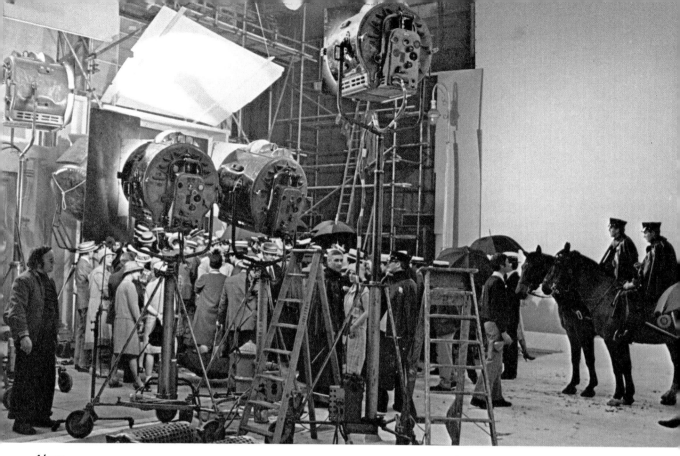

Above
An outdoor sequence shot in the studio. The actors wait to begin the crowd scene outside the funeral parlor.

Opposite above
Michelle Phillips and Nureyev walk away from the tent designed by Philip Harrison for *The Sheik* sequence. The 60 foot palm trees were imported and buried in concrete to withstand the wind.

approach,' he said. 'There's acting and there's the sort of non-professional behaviourism – fooling around and champagne on the set and all the old Holywood nonsense which Russell sends up in the *Monsieur Beaucaire* scenes. I find that very disconcerting.'

To Nureyev's eye the relaxed and free-wheeling approach of the other school obviously looked sloppy; while its exponents must have found the tight, concentrated rhythms of a dancer puzzling. At the start there were, for instance, visible differences in approach between Nureyev and Michelle Phillips. She came from a totally different background from his. Born and bred in California, she started her career as a rock singer with an American group, the Mommas and Poppas. In 1969 the group disbanded and she took a course with a Los Angeles acting workshop. She made her film debut as the gangster's girl-friend in *Dillinger:* Russell saw her performance and thought her blend of sexy charm and toughness would be just right for his conception of Rambova. 'I asked him to dinner at a Mexican restaurant,' she relates. 'When he arrived I had my hair done up in braids as I thought Rambova's would have been. I didn't want to leave everything to chance.' She got the part.

Before shooting started she made a fascinating discovery. 'I noticed in a newspaper report that Valentino's funeral was organised by Rambova's sister, Katherine Peterson of Pasadena. I rang 'information' and there she still was, now aged 85. I talked to her for several hours and she remembered lots of

APERTURE FILMS LIMITED

DAILY PROGRESS REPORT No. 18

WEDNESDAY,

PRODUCTION "VALENTINO"   DIRECTOR KEN RUSSELL   DATE 1st September, 1976

STARTED 12.8.76   FINISHING DATE 3.12.76

		SCENE NUMBERS	
ESTIMATED DAYS	88	LOCATION OF WORK/SET	COMPLETED
DAYS TO DATE	18	EMI STUDIOS, Stage 4	
REMAINING DAYS	72	for	PART 31pt.
DAYS OVER	2	INT. TENT	
DAYS UNDER			

TIME

CALL on set	8.30
1st SET UP COMPLETED	11.45
LUNCH FROM	1.00
TO	2.00
UNIT DISMISSED	6.45
TOTAL HOURS	

SCRIPT SCENES

	SCRIPT		EXTRA		RETAKES	
	NUMBER	MINUTES	NUMBER	MINUTES	NUMBER	MINUTES
PREVIOUSLY TAKEN	9	19.31			1	—
TAKEN TO-DAY	—	2.12				
TAKEN TO DATE Deleted	9 2	21.43			1	
TO BE TAKEN	77	118.17	DAILY AVERAGES. OVERALL:			1.12
TOTAL SCRIPT SCENES	88	140.00	STUDIO: 1.22		LOCATION:	1.11

ACTION PROPS AND EFFECTS

2 WIND MACHINES
PLAYBACK

SLATE NUMBERS

99 - 102

SET UPS: 4

STILLS

	B & W	COLOUR
PREVIOUSLY TAKEN	66	72
TAKEN TO-DAY	2	2
TAKEN TO DATE	68	74

CONTRACT ARTISTES

NAME	W	S/B	RE	CALL	ARR	D'SS'D
RUDOLF NUREYEV	15			7.45	8.15	6.45
MICHELLE PHILLIPS	13			7.30	7.30	6.45
JENNIE LINDEN	1			2.30	2.30	6.45
COSTUME FITTINGS						
BILL McKINNEY				12.00	12.00	3.00
DUDLEY SUTTON				10.00	10.00	12.00
CHARLES FARRELL				11.00	11.00	12.00
MURRAY SALEM				12.00	12.00	1.00
D. COSTELLO				10.00	10.00	12.00
DIANA WESTON				11.00	11.00	12.30
MAGGY MAXWELL				12.00	12.00	1.00

CROWDS

Stand-Ins:
M. CLARK (2 day)
A. PRESTON
D. HART

Extras:
(Auditions/
Fittings)
4 x
4 x

ADDITIONAL CREWS

PICTURE — FILM FOOTAGES — SOUND

WASTE	RES'VE & N.G.	PRINT	TOTAL		PRINT	MASTER ROLLS	¼" TAPE
2786	22400	28533	53719	PREVIOUSLY USED		49	29400
240	1490	4940	6670	USED TO-DAY		4	2400
3026	23890	33473	60389	TOTALS TO DATE		53	31800
SHORT ENDS:	2340				WASTE:		

REMARKS

ON HIRE: (Samuelsons) 1 DAY
1 BL CAMERA with full complement of lenses, and magazines.

MEDICAL REPORT
Dr. Collins visited Keith Pamplin (Boom Operator), on set to treat him for an ear condition.

PRODUCTION MANAGER

Anthony Dowell, as Nijinsky, looks on while
Gillian Gregory rehearses Nureyev in a tango.

Robert Chartoff with Gillian Gregory the
choreographer.

Opposite
A typical shooting schedule for *Valentino.*

small details. Rambova died only five years ago, so many
people have memories of her – mostly negative, because she
wasn't the most popular girl in the world. At fifteen she had
run away from Denver, Colorado, bought a sailor suit and
sailed to Europe as a marine. On her return she joined a ballet
company.

'After she parted from Valentino she married a Spanish
nobleman; some of his family were executed in the Civil War
and Rambova was supposed to be next on the condemned list.
She was smuggled out of Spain, went to Egypt, deciphered
some tomb inscriptions, wrote two books about them and then
returned to America where she looked after heroin addicts in
New York. She had quite a busy life. She was a lesbian, but I
think she was about as asexual as you can get; her real turn-ons
were artistic.'

Michelle Phillips's concept of her role ('Rambova was highly
cultured and incredibly intelligent and she dominated her
husband at every turn') combined with her Los Angeles trained
style of working, presented problems for Nureyev who
admitted freely, 'I found it difficult to adjust to playing
opposite her.' But the disparities were resolved, as the final
performance showed. The contrast between the two tempera-
ments may even have lent some extra nuances to the strikingly
similar differences between the personalities of the original
Italian-born Valentino and his wife from Salt Lake City.

Interesting contrasts of acting technique also became apparent as the shooting progressed. 'Valentino was very aware of the camera as every movie actor must be,' Nureyev remarks. 'In any case Russell demands a larger-than-life style of acting. At the start I thought I shouldn't move so much; but then the camera picks up a feeling of restriction. You have to be as free and natural in front of it as possible. It's not only a question of you liking the camera, but also of the camera liking you. The response must be two-way.' Leslie Caron takes the same view. 'You would be surprised how much you have to be aware of every movement. That's all-important in a film. In the frame you only get fragments of the body, never the whole thing, and the smallest gesture takes on enormous importance.' Seymour Cassell gives the opposite advice. 'You just have to play the scene and forget the camera; the director will look after you.'

Nureyev on the other hand brought to his acting the same watchful intensity as he does to his dancing. 'I found him very patient, very conscientious – humble almost,' said Leslie Caron afterwards. 'Before we started people said to me: "Oh my God – Ken Russell *and* Nureyev, that's going to be horrendous!" But I found them both very exciting to work with. Rudi's a natural learner, he listens. If it's about dancing, he knows better than you do and there he can't be taught; but if it's about something he doesn't know, you can tell him and he accepts it and he'll do it again and again until he's satisfied. He has genius – you can see the wheels working.'

Leslie Caron, who started her career as a dancer in France, plays Nazimova, (Rambova's friend and another influence on Valentino), who started her career as an actress in Russia. 'She had been quite well-known there in her youth and she worked in London for a few years before going to America,' said Caron. 'I remember seeing the house in Los Angeles where she had lived – she had called it 'The Garden of Alla', Alla being her Christian name. She's been made more extravagant in the film than she really was, but I love her character; she was totally insane and misguided but very generous and alive, and even intelligent in an intuitive way – a really warm theatrical personality.'

There were plenty of theatrical personalities on the *Valentino* set, and none more so than Nureyev. But both actors and crew, seem to have ended up with respect for the star. Huntz Hall, a veteran of 138 pictures who, curiously, made his debut on Broadway with the real Nazimova – as a three month old baby – called Nureyev 'the most professional actor I have worked with' and even 'the nicest gentleman I have ever met.' Carol Kane, the American actress who plays the starlet in *Valentino* was touchingly grateful to him for his help in her dancing scene with him. 'I was terrified. I burst out crying. He just smiled and said "You'll never make a ballerina if you cry".' Jonathan Benson adds his impression 'The strength of Nureyev's character and his intelligence created in the film a

Above
Carol Kane as the starlet.

Opposite
Michelle Phillips in one of the original period dresses that Shirley Russell found for the film.

Nureyev as the matador.

character which is different from the way it was written – stronger, with a lot of integrity. And he catches Valentino's animal quality in the silent scenes.' Seymour Cassell, brought up in the tough school of Cassavetes, was somewhat shocked that Nureyev had to learn how to swing a punch, but could not help admiring his physical shape in the boxing ring compared with his own. ('After all, you've had two children,' remarked his wife consolingly.)

Other characters make shorter appearances, among them Felicity Kendal, British television star, as June Mathis ('Russell and Nureyev share the honest characteristic of subordinating everything and everybody to their objective, without the pretences most people use'); Alfred Marks, well-known London actor, as Richard Rowland, Valentino's first director; William Hootkins, a London-based Texan padded out as 'Fatty'. They add up to make an international macedoine of talent with one remarkable characteristic. Many of them are cast contrariwise. Ballet-trained Leslie Caron acts but does not dance; singer Michelle Phillips dances but does not sing; British actors play Americans; an English dancer impersonates a Russian one; and finally, a great Russian star reincarnates a great Italian star. This ultimate transformation symbolises the special Ken Russell wizardry. Through a recipe mixing boldness and tenacity, imagination and perspicuity, decisive direction and sustained performance-power, a spell has been conjured up. The fusion of Valentino and Nureyev produces a potent magic.

Cast List

Rudolph Valentino	Rudolf Nureyev
Alla Nazimova	Leslie Caron
Natasha Rambova	Michelle Phillips
Starlet	Carol Kane
June Mathis	Felicity Kendal
George Ullman	Seymour Cassell
Jesse Lasky	Huntz Hall
Richard Rowland	Alfred Marks
Joseph Schenck	David De Keyser
Billie Streeter	Linda Thorson
Marjorie Tain	Leland Palmer
Angus McBride	Lindsay Kemp
Rory O'Neil	Peter Vaughan
Nijinsky	Anthony Dowell
Lorna Sinclair	Penelope Milford
Bianca de Saulles	June Bolton
Jack de Saulles	Robin Clark
Fatty	William Hootkins
Sidney Olcott	John Justin
Baron Long	Anton Diffring
Marsha Lee	Nicolette Marvin
Agnes Ayres	Jennie Linden
Studio Guard	Percy Herbert
Willie	Dudley Sutton
Girl in Tango Sequence	Christine Carlson
George Melford	Don Fellows
Policeman	Bill McKinney
Hooker	Marcella Markham
Cop	John Alderson
Pretty Girl	Elizabeth Bagley
Drunk	Charles Farrell
Harry Fischbeck	Hal Galili
The Sheik	Richard Le Parmentier
Ray C. Smallwood	Scott Miller
Assistant Director	Burnell Tucker
Make-Up Girl	Diana Von Fossen
Electrician	Ray Jewers
Vagrant	Murray Salem
Lady at Maxim's	Mildred Shay
1st Whore	Deirdre Costello
2nd Whore	Diana Weston
Assistant Director	Mark Baker
Girl Friend	Amy Farber

Technical Credits

Executive Producer	Robert Chartoff
Director	Ken Russell
Screenplay	Ken Russell
Associate Producer	Harry Benn
Production Manager	Peter Price
Director of Photography	Peter Suschitsky
Camera Operator	Ronnie Taylor
Art Director	Philip Harrison
Editor	Stuart Baird
Costume Designer	Shirley Russell
Assistant Director	Jonathan Benson
Continuity	Zelda Barron
Sound Mixer	John Mitchell
Set Dresser	Ian Whittaker
Location Manager	Richard Green
Wardrobe Master	Richard Pointing
Wardrobe Mistress	Rebecca Breed
Chief Make-Up	Peter Robb-King
Chief Hairdresser	Colin Jamison
Production Accountant	Len Cave
Production Secretary	Pat Pennelegion
Casting Director	Maude Spector
Choreographer	Gillian Gregory
Property Master	Ray Traynor
Construction Manager	Jeffrey Woodbridge
Dialogue Coach	Marcella Markham
Stills Photographer	Barry Peake
Publicist	Brian Doyle

THE VALENTINO STORY

For the sake of narrative clarity, the order of some of the scenes in the film have been changed in this chapter.

It is August 1926: the heat is stifling. In the centre of McBride's Funeral Church in New York a figure lies in an open coffin. It is Rudolph Valentino, the great screen lover, victim of overwrought nerves and peritonitis. His sudden illness had been followed with shocked fascination by half the world, his death had come as a thunderbolt. Outside the church a hundred thousand hysterical fans struggle to view the body, pressing against the bullet-proof windows. Inside the only sound is some business-like voices. Three of Hollywood's top film executives are grouped round the coffin – Jesse Lasky (Paramount), Joseph Schenck (United Artists), Richard Rowland (MGM) – talking to the funeral parlor's owner, McBride. They are worried men. Will the corpse last long enough to get the distribution contracts on his last film? What effect will his death have on the box-office?

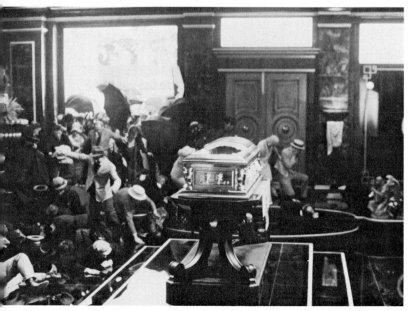

The crowds outside are becoming more and more impatient.

Frustration and resentment build up as they are kept from viewing their idol. Suddenly a camera flash shatters a glass window and a mass of screaming fans falls into the room, some cut, others bruised and shaken.

While the executives slip out to safety through a back door, McBride and his assistants rush forward to restore order. In the calm that follows, the brass doors swing open just wide enough to admit some of Valentino's close friends and associates. They are quickly followed by the ever-present sensation-seeking newsmen and press photographers, who vie with each other to get the best story.

One of them recognizes June Mathis, a screen-writer who had helped Valentino at the start of his career. Another descends on Bianca de Saulles, a tiny figure sitting alone, tearfully clutching a small bunch of violets. 'Say, sister, you look kinda cute all alone with your posy. Make a nice picture . . . How about a big smile?' The journalist pumps her memory for an exclusive story in return for keeping her identity a secret from his colleagues. 'To think you knew him when he was a nobody; nothin' but a gigolo! You were his first love . . . Now smile through your tears. Great, kid, great!'

Every afternoon Maxim's tea-room is crowded with fashionable New York ladies. Its particular attraction is the young men who can be hired as dancing partners. One day the manageress, Billie Streeter, arrives early with Bianca. They are confronted with an extraordinary sight – two men dancing together. It is the most accomplished of her 'taxi-dancers' giving a tango lesson to the famous Russian Ballet star, Nijinsky.

They stare in amazement as the lesson ends and Nijinsky finishes with a dazzling series of spins and leaps round the floor. As he is introduced to Bianca, Nijinsky notices an intimate smile pass between her and Valentino.

Billie relates the incident on the telephone to her current lover, Bianca's
husband, Jack de Saulles. As she begins
changing for the evening, she describes
Valentino's dance with 'the fairy'. From
their conversation it is evident that Jack
is disturbed by his wife's relationship
with the young gigolo.

She then lines up her taxi-dancers for
inspection before the customers arrive.

She looks at them with good-natured
contempt as she comes to the end where
Valentino is standing. 'I've seen better
line-ups in the police gazette. The only
one to cut any ice is Saint Rudolpho
here.' She circles him possessively, her
face a few inches from his, adding 'And
you've got to circulate more. Lay off the
de Saulles dame and give some of the old
broads a whirl. They tip better . . .'

Billie has tipped off Bianca's husband and he arrives at Maxim's to find his wife dancing with Valentino. De Saulles strides across the room to his wife. 'No more tea-time hops with dagos for you, baby . . . blow, pretty boy!' Valentino manages to keep control of himself. De Saulles starts to lead his wife off the floor. 'Waltzin' around with wops is one thing . . . but with a pansy – Jesus!' 'Sir, I am an artist,' replies Valentino icily. 'And I say that any guy who dances with another guy is a powder puff!' retorts de Saulles.

Valentino looks to Billie for support – unaware that it is she who betrayed him. She responds by firing him. Insultingly de Saulles stuffs a $20 tip into his pocket.

Valentino is momentarily taken aback but recovers control and flourishes the note, announcing that he is now a paying customer and would like the best table. He is willingly plied with champagne.

A few days later Valentino, out of work again, is cooking supper for Bianca and her little son in his squalid tenement room. He tells her of his dreams of buying an orange farm and bringing his mother to America. There Bianca would be safe from her vengeful husband.

Bianca knows that her husband is unfaithful to her. Grief and anger overpower her equally. One day she is out in the car when the face of her husband appears at the window. He is mocking her in her unhappiness. Suddenly she produces a gun from under her furs and points it at him with trembling hands. He doesn't believe she is serious. But she is desperate. 'You're not taking him from me!' she cries, and empties the gun into his face. He falls dead.

Fatty, a popular comedian, is throwing a party at a night club in Los Angeles. The band strikes up for the cabaret. Valentino enters, executes a few steps and turns to greet his partner, Marjorie Tain. As she fumbles with the bead curtain it becomes clear that she is hopelessly drunk. Valentino tries to guide her through their routine, but a storm of catcalls drives her from the floor.

Furious, Valentino turns and fixes his eyes on Fatty. He advances on him like a panther, then pounces on his starlet companion. 'Madam, permit me to complete your dance card,' he asks with feigned politeness, then deftly whirls her onto the floor where he guides her into an erotic tango. He finally jumps onto the table and, executing a defiant dance under Fatty's very nose, ends by deliberately kicking a full glass into his lap. The guests are amused, but Valentino is out of a job again.

On the suggestion of the starlet, Valentino uses his dancing connections to
obtain small parts in some Hollywood
movies. He has been spotted by June
Mathis, an influential screen-writer. She
is looking for a hero for her new film,
The Four Horsemen of the Apocalypse, and
she persuades Richard Rowland of
MGM to give him a test, showing some
clips of his previous film parts, most of
which are slapstick comedy.

Unaware of the type she is looking
for, Valentino tries to impress her by
dressing up like the current American
film heroes – wholesome, open-air kids.
'You see, I am as Yankee as the next
man!' June can hardly conceal her
amusement as she tells him 'My hero is
to be a gaucho from Argentina with a
taste for the tango.' Instantly Valentino
changes style, bows low as he kisses her
hand, and introduces himself by his full
resounding Italian name.

June is viewing the first rushes of *The Four Horsemen of the Apocalypse*, when the door of the theatre unexpectedly bursts open. News of Valentino has reached Alla Nazimova, Hollywood's most outrageous and avant garde director. She strides in with Rowland and Natasha Rambova, her protégée, and they watch the black and white images of the gaucho dancing an electrifying tango on the screen.

The effect on Nazimova of Valentino's elegance and passion is immediate. She is entranced and paces the room. 'Like a tiger,' she exclaims. 'He moves like a tiger. What grace! What sensuality!' She has no need to listen to June's recommendations. Her decision to have Valentino in her next film, *Camille*, is already made. She is impatient to find him.

Observed by a film crew, four horsemen in fantastic costume thunder across the Californian desert. Suddenly their headlong charge is arrested by the arrival across their path of an open car. It contains Nazimova with Rambova and some of their friends, looking for Valentino. Nazimova marches round the location, oblivious of the havoc she is causing. She even imperiously accosts an unfortunate young man whose face is hidden by a gas-mask. The distraught director, Rex Ingram, warns them that Valentino is in no mood to receive visitors, but they carry on undeterred.

Finally they find him, in a soldier's uniform, alone in a bomb crater. He holds a letter announcing the death of his mother. His thoughts are far away in Italy. Even Nazimova is moved.

Valentino has become famous after his success in *The Four Horsemen of the Apocalypse* and Nazimova has cast him to play opposite herself in her new film *Camille;* he will be Armand, the lover of the Lady of the Camelias. The production has been designed by Rambova in the latest style, from the scene where Armand arrives at Camille's funeral, to the flashback when he woos her.

Rambova, the eccentric step-daughter of a wealthy tycoon, had adopted a Russian name for a tour with a ballet troupe. She is as determined as she is talented and has fixed her sights on Valentino. He is captivated by her strange charm and falls completely under her spell. On the Californian sands where his new picture, *The Sheik*, is being filmed, they lie in the sun discussing the future. Rambova has big ideas for his artistic career. She consults the bones of Meselope, an Egyptian priest, which she always carries with her for spiritual guidance. The hesitant Valentino is reassured.

Work on filming *The Sheik* is over for the day and Valentino is left alone on the set with Rambova. She taunts him for acting in such popular movies and then lures him into the Sheik's tent with a seductive strip-tease dance. Valentino is hypnotized by her beauty. 'I'd give half my kingdom for you to finish it,' he cries in the language of the Sheik, as he follows her eagerly. She slips out of her last garment and poses, provocatively naked, on the divan where the Sheik is to make his conquest the next day. Valentino clambers out of his robes and tries to make love to her among the oriental cushions. But she coolly evades his embraces, reminding him that he is still married. She suggests a divorce. Valentino, though disappointed and frustrated, is delighted at the prospect of being married to her.

Rambova is always practical. 'Please get dressed. You look silly standing there in nothing but a turban.' As she hands him his costume she scolds, 'You promised to fold it neatly for the big rape scene tomorrow.' He complies and meekly follows her out of the tent. There is no question who is going to be in command when they get married.

The screen Sheik is a very different character. In the film he is shown fiercely wreaking his will on the near-swooning heroine, Agnes Ayres. He throws her roughly on the divan and leaps on her defenceless body like a wildcat. She struggles in vain as the title comes up on the screen: 'Lie still, you little fool!'

The screen magic works on an audience of hysterical fans, whose voices rise in a crescendo: 'It's his eyes! It's his mouth! He's so masterful, I want to die in his arms. Take me, Rudy, take me!' Alone among the packed rows of adorers, June Mathis sits almost in tears. She too is carried away by romantic emotion. In a dream she imagines herself swept up in the strong arms of the Sheik and carried away on his white stallion.

Valentino has become the plaything of
Nazimova and Rambova. Against the
idiosyncratic decor of Nazimova's apart-
ment, he impersonates for her camera
the Greek faun immortalized by the
dancer Nijinsky. The two women have
dressed themselves up as a pair of sexy
nymphs. Nazimova takes most of the
pictures as Valentino and Rambova
adopt erotic poses. They are carried
away by their make-believe love-
making, and as they lie entwined on the
floor, the jealous Nazimova gets some
compromising photographs. Somehow
the pictures find their way into a newspaper which publishes them with an
article on Valentino's impending divorce. Rambova suspects that she has
been betrayed by her friend and furious-
ly announces that she is leaving her. 'I
didn't plan it that way, believe me,'
pleads Nazimova. 'No . . . it's time to
change partners.' The affair is over, and
Rambova drives off with Valentino to
get married in Mexico.

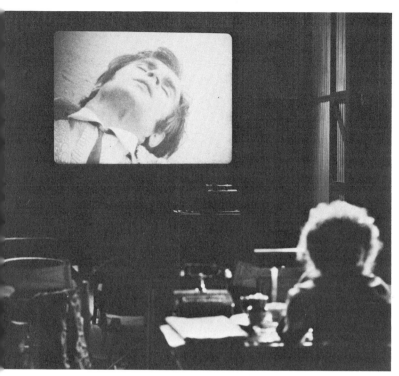

In his new film Valentino stars as a Spanish matador. June Mathis is sitting watching the rushes on her private screen when a colleague hurries in with the bad news that Valentino is in jail charged with bigamy and will only be released on a bail of $10,000. Appalled, June turns for help to Lasky, boss of the studio. She finds him in his study contemplating his favourite pet, a prize gorilla. 'What are you doing about getting Valentino out of jail?' she asks. 'Nothing.' says Lasky laconically. 'But he's your biggest star. $10,000 is chicken feed to the studio — you made a fortune out of him.' Lasky is unmoved. 'Why spend $10,000 to get him out when we are getting a million dollars worth of free publicity with him inside? The more the press knock the boy, the bigger the box office.' June glares at the gorilla behind his bars and walks out in disgust.

As soon as the newly married pair return from Mexico, Valentino is arrested by the Californian police. His divorce is not considered final under state law. In prison Valentino has been recognized and instantly becomes the object of abuse and taunts. Whores grab his arms through the bars as they try to tear his clothes off. His fellow prisoners hurl obscenities and lewd suggestions at him. Finally, one of the warders mixes a diuretic drug in a mug of coffee and gives it to Valentino. The whole prison rocks with amusement as Valentino desperately tries not to wet his pants. 'Any minute now, fellas!' cries the jailor in delight. As his bladder gives way, Valentino climbs the bars in anguish, babbling an incoherent prayer.

Unknown to him, June Mathis has stood bail for Valentino. He returns to Hollywood determined on a path of action dictated by Rambova. They confront Lasky on the set of a Western and demand, not just double Valentino's salary, but script approval as well. Lasky refuses adamantly and becomes threatening when Valentino tells him that he will find work elsewhere. 'The only work you'll find, my boy, is waiting on tables in a pizza parlor. Your contract has two years to go and if you so much as take a pratfall in a Mexican two-reeler, I'll slap an injunction on your ass!'

Retorting that he could use a vacation, Valentino slips his car into gear and leaves Lasky coughing in a cloud of dust as it disappears.

Looking like tousled happy beach-combers, their hair bleached by the sun, Valentino and Rambova are enjoying their enforced vacation by the sea.

They resent the appearance of a figure carrying a briefcase who comes awkwardly across the beach to meet them. He introduces himself as George Ullman, a representative of Mineralava Toiletries. Relieved that he is not another newspaperman, they listen to his strange proposition.

He offers them more money than they have ever earned in return for a dancing tour to promote his company's wares. 'An exercise in interpretive dance – with a few kind words for the product thrown in for a finale.' Valentino agrees but Rambova hesitates and consults her fortune-telling bones. After an anxious moment, the answer comes: 'Yes!' The new venture is toasted in champagne.

One of the routines that Valentino and Rambova perform is a tango in front of a giant bottle of Mineralava. The predominantly female audience adore it. Their rapturous applause disproves Lasky's prediction that, off-screen, Valentino would be dead and buried. Dutifully Valentino plugs the company that had 'made possible our appearance here tonight,' and Rambova (step-daughter of a cosmetics tycoon) lends loyal support. 'I prefer Mineralava to all other beauty products. Including Daddy's!'

Ullman is watching the performance delightedly from a stage box. Suddenly a voice behind him makes him jump. It is Lasky who wants to make another deal with the Valentinos. He agrees to all Valentino's terms and this time he is even ready to agree to the condition demanded by Rambova — that she should be officially engaged as artistic director.

Under Rambova's guidance, Valentino is making an 'artistic' film, an eighteenth century romance, *Monsieur Beaucaire*. He is the epitome of the period hero, a dandy in satin kneebreeches who can take on a whole army single handed.

The atmosphere is electric. The director Sidney Olcott, is nearly distracted. Rambova's assumption of the role of artistic director has been a disaster. Time and time again shooting is held up because of her interruptions.

Waiting for her love-scene with Valentino, his co-star Lorna passes the time by reading a fan magazine, while the lighting cameraman — exasperatedly awaiting new instructions — peers over her shoulder.

The director and Rambova sit side by side urging on a love scene like rival boxing coaches. 'Swoon, Lorna!' 'More restraint, Rudy! – Roll your eyes, damn you!' 'Now close your eyes!' As Valentino and his screen countess draw apart from their embrace, something falls into his brocaded lap. It is a large pink powder puff, dropped by a cynical electrician. Rambova demands that the culprit should come forward, but nobody moves. Furious, she walks off the set, while Valentino hesitates. 'If you want to win back the respect of the crew, you'll have to screw that little whore Lorna!' Rambova shouts back at him mockingly.

Valentino takes Rambova's advice literally during a lunch break. Lorna is in a delirium of happiness and takes off on a fantasy trip. Valentino is totally detached: he finds her ardours amusing and worries about getting back to the set on time.

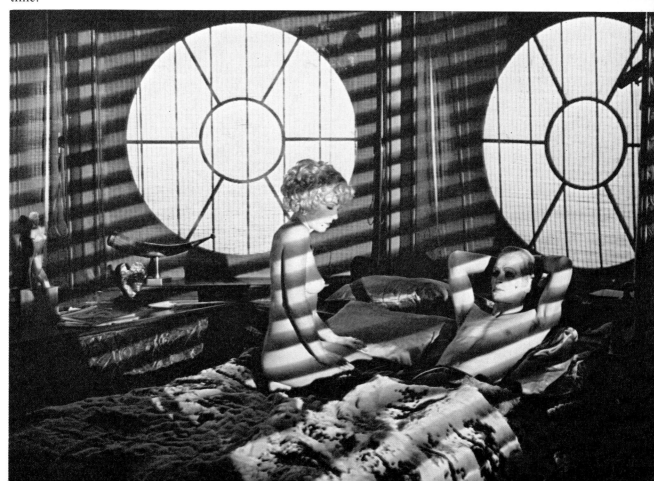

When Valentino arrives back home, he
finds an upset and tearful Rambova with
a grim-faced Ullman. His immediate
thought is that Rambova must have
heard about his interlude with Lorna.
But her anxieties are much more far-
reaching. Ullman, now Valentino's
manager, has brought the sought-after
contract with United Artists. But Ullman has been spelling out the small
print, and it becomes clear that Rambova is virtually barred from the set. Valentino and Rambova are appalled by the
implications. Ullman tries to soothe
them saying that she will merely not be
expected to participate in any stage of
production. 'Impossible!' exclaims Valentino, as he snatches the contract and
tears it up. 'We don't need United
Artists. We don't need anyone.'

Ullman picks up his things and leaves, while Valentino tries to comfort Rambova. 'Hollywood's killing me!' she complains. 'What's to stop us getting that orange grove?' suggests Valentino. 'I've still got my Diploma of Agriculture.' 'I'd hoped destiny would promise us a richer fate!' Rambova is resentful, suspicious and despairing.

With their future uncertain, Valentino and Rambova consult the spirit world. Eyes shut, hands joined, they crouch over a crystal ball. 'What is our destiny to be?' Rambova asks. 'Are we to continue to work together?' The table begins to shake. Rambova is becoming more and more worked up. 'We are to stay in films, but work separately — yes?' she asks excitedly.

As they wait for spiritual affirmation, the sound of voices comes through the window: 'You are the spirit that moves the universe! You are the zephyr of passion!' Rambova is trembling. 'Are we to remain together — are we? Are we?' 'Of course we shall,' says Valentino, trying to calm her, 'I'll arrange anything you need. I just want us to be together.' He takes her in his arms passionately and starts to make love to her as she lies across the table. The chanting chorus outside grows louder as Rambova bursts into hysterical laughter.

The voices come from a crowd of fans in the garden: 'You – are the food of love! You – are the thrill of surrender! You – are the dream that intoxicates!'

'Jesus Christ!', Valentino exclaims when Rambova will not respond to his passion. 'Aren't you just!' she rejoins mockingly, as she listens to the worshippers outside. She can stand it no longer. The relationship has been destroyed for ever.

Rambova is now independent and has made a film of her own, called *What Price Beauty?* Valentino too has made a new movie, *The Son of the Sheik,* but he is unwell. The evening before a reception to promote it, he takes Ullman to see Rambova's film. They come out depressed. 'It was terrible,' says Valentino. 'I'm sorry for her.' 'Don't worry,' says Ullman. 'We leave for Hollywood tomorrow night. It's important you see your doctor.'

They wander off down the dimly lit street, only to be accosted by a prostitute. 'Fancy a good time?' she asks, offering to take them both on at the same time. 'I envy you, madam,' says Valentino wryly. 'I myself don't seem capable of sustaining even one effort for very long. Come on, George, let's get a drink.' Ullman tries to detain him, reminding him that he is not supposed to be touching anything but milk, but without success. They find themselves in a nightclub. The prostitute leads them to a table near the dance floor.

A group of girls dressed as pink powder puffs run in, dancing and singing,

> 'Oh Rudy, what have you done to the U.S. male?
> We liked him better when his cheeks were pale.
> Think it's time I took a powder
> From Rudy, the pink powder puff!'

The prostitute claims that the chorus is based on a newspaper article. Valentino rushes out. 'You knew about that article!' he accuses Ullman. 'How dare he insult my manhood. I shall challenge him.' 'For God's sake, we don't fight duels in America,' protests Ullman. 'I shall challenge him to a boxing match.' Valentino issues the challenge at a press conference. It is not seriously accepted by the journalist — an ex-heavyweight boxer — until he antagonizes Valentino to the point where the star punches him.

The boxing match has been turned into a publicity stunt. Guests in evening dress dance round the ring and pack the stands. Valentino appears. His opponent, huge but gone-to-seed, hasn't even bothered to change from his office suit. 'Ladies and gentlemen,' calls the referee, 'we are presenting a contest between Rory O'Neil of the New York Evening News in the red corner, and Rudy Valentino of Hollywood in the pink corner.' There are cheers and laughter as the bell rings.

O'Neil begins to punch Valentino round the ring, doing what he likes with him. Ullman and June Mathis are worried, not only about the outcome of the fight, but by the damage that is being done to Valentino's face and reputation. By the third round Valentino is almost finished, but so is O'Neil, who has been swigging whisky between rounds. Suddenly Valentino rallies and lands a blow on O'Neil's chin; he falls and never really recovers. Before the end of the round, Valentino is declared the winner.

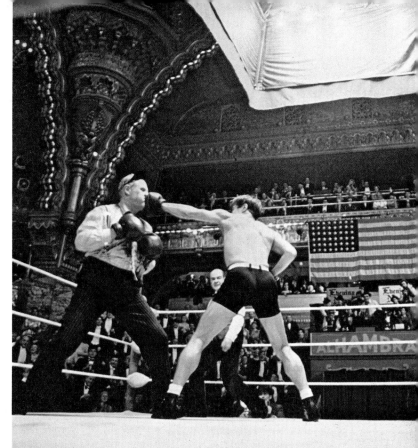

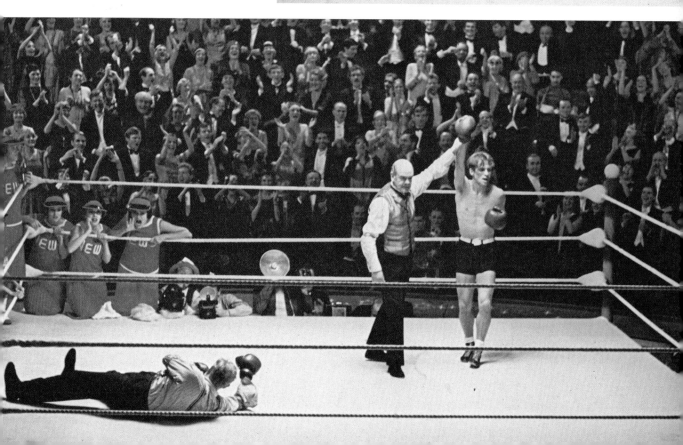

Valentino and O'Neil go off to celebrate. In another contest – a drinking competition – each sits behind a stack of empty glasses, adding to them steadily. June Mathis is encouraging but anxious, knowing that Valentino is on a strict diet. Soon both men are far gone. O'Neil passes out, and Valentino is the winner again. With difficulty he rises to his feet. 'I feel I have vindicated my honour and my manhood!'

He staggers back to his room, half-falling as he feels a stab of pain in his stomach. Still elated, he begins to dance across the floor towards a bowl of oranges. As he puts out his hand to take one, he collapses. A single orange rolls across the carpet, just out of reach, like the dream of happiness which escapes him to the end.

McBride's Funeral Parlor is filled to the roof with flowers, a theatrical setting for Valentino's last appearance. The mourners make carefully stage-managed entrances. Nazimova arrives, acting the heroic tragedy-queen; her 20 foot train of white camelias is carried by a bevy of starlets. As they drape it over the coffin, she sinks down upon it dramatically – repeating the movement to please the photographers. Rambova sails in beneath a black veil, pausing long enough to give an interview to the journalists. 'The winds of destiny tore us apart. But if his lips may never touch mine again, at least I can embrace his spirit.'

'Don't worry', Nazimova whispers into her ear, 'Other lips await you in your young life. Lips that warned you this would happen.' 'Perhaps it's true. I only know that there will never be another Valentino. There'll never be another remotely like him. He was a god.'